JF
NOSTLINGER, C.   13.12.85
Brainbox sorts it
out   DERBY JUNIOR

14   1989

17   MAY 1988

1   3 JUL 1988

CW01095403

17 APR 1986   14 JAN 1987   -3 SEP 1988

20 JUN 1986   -7 FEB 1987   6 OCT 1988

WITHDRAWN FROM... NOT FOR SALE

31 OCT 1989

12 JUN 1990

29 JUN 1990

31 JUL 1990

7 MAR 1992   27 OCT 1990

25 FEB 1991

20 JUL 1991

BRAINBOX SORTS IT OUT

Christine Nostlinger

BRAINBOX SORTS IT OUT

Translated by Anthea Bell

DERBYSHIRE
COUNTY LIBRARY
13 DEC 1985
DERBY CENTRA

IS JFic

WITHDRAWN FROM STOCK FOR SALE

Andersen Press · London

First published in 1985 by
Andersen Press Limited,
19-21 Conway Street,
London W.1.

All rights reserved. No part of this publication may be
reproduced, stored in a retrieval system, or transmitted in any
form or by any means, electronic, mechanical, photocopying,
recording or otherwise, without the written permission of the
publisher.

© 1981 by Jugend und Volk Verlagsgesellschaft m.b.H.
First published in English in 1985.
This translation ©1985 by Andersen Press Limited.
Originally published in German as *Der Denker greift ein*
by Jugend und Volk Verlagsgesellschaft m.b.H, Vienna,
Austria.

British Library Cataloguing in Publication Data

Nostlinger, Christine
    Brainbox sorts it out.
    I. Title II. Der Denker greift ein. *English*
    823'.914[J]   PZ7

    ISBN 0-86264-096-2

Printed and bound in Great Britain
by Anchor Brendon Limited, Tiptree, Essex.

Chapter 1

in which nothing much happens, but we get to know the most important people in the story.

Otto had short, bristly, carrotty hair and great big sticking-out ears. He was tall and he was thin, and his skin was covered with freckles. Not dear little freckles, the sort people admire on a girl's snub nose. Otto was brown and white all over, like a spotted dog. As if he'd been standing near a painter who was using a spray gun to put brown paint on a wall. There were some truly huge freckles on Otto. He had one on his left cheek the same shape as Africa, with Cairo and the Cape of Good Hope and all. And there was a giant freckle just to the right of his navel. It was heart-shaped, a heart the size of your thumbnail, with a tiny stalk in the middle so that it looked like the Ace of Spades in a pack of playing cards.

Everyone in the class called Otto Ace, because of this freckle. (That is, everyone except Thomas Huber, who called him Ass instead, or sometimes Silly Ass, but Thomas Huber doesn't count. He and Otto were deadly enemies at the time.)

Michael was very tall and very thin too, but his skin was the same colour all over: pale brown, like milky coffee. Michael's grandfather had been a negro, a soldier in the United States Army of Occupation. So Michael's mother was half negro, and Michael was quarter negro.

Michael had curly black hair, and dark brown eyes with long, thick lashes. All the girls agreed that he was gorgeous. Moreover, he usually dressed as if he were just off to the opera, with a bow tie on, and a white shirt, and a blue

5

blazer. He had a folded handkerchief in his breast pocket and creases in the legs of his grey trousers. Sometimes he wore casual clothes, meaning a white suede jacket that was so grand nobody dared to touch him, in case they left dirty fingermarks on the beautiful white leather. Michael never spoke in Viennese dialect, either. He was always being held up to the class as a fine example of the correct use of their native tongue. Which was true: even when Michael said, 'Oh, shit!' as he often did, he pronounced it beautifully. On account of being so posh, Michael was known as His Nibs, or just Nibs, to everyone in the class. (Even including Thomas Huber.)

Daniel was short and stout and fair and rosy. He was stout, but nobody ever saw him eat much. And his cheeks were rosy although he never got any fresh air of his own free will. And he was always top of the class. But no one ever saw him studying much, or paying particular attention in lessons. Daniel usually just sat there with his eyes half closed, sucking his thumb. You might have thought he was about to fall asleep. Now and then the teachers thought so too. 'Wake up, Daniel!' they would say, in friendly tones, because teachers nearly always speak in friendly tones to a person who is top of the class. On such occasions, Daniel would take his thumb out of his mouth and murmur, 'I'm not asleep, I'm thinking.'

He didn't say what he was thinking about, and if anyone asked him he would say, evasively, 'Just thinking.'

Daniel was usually called Brainbox.

Brainbox, His Nibs and Ace were friends. They had always been friends. They had gone to nursery school together, and to primary school, and now they were in the same class again at secondary school. His Nibs sat next to Ace, and Brainbox sat in front of them.

Lizzie was one of them in a way, too, because she had been

to the same nursery school and the same primary school as well. This was how she got to sit next to Brainbox and have good marks; she copied from him. Or if she couldn't copy from him, say in maths, where there was an A Group and a B Group for maths tests, and Brainbox did the A Group test and Lizzie did the B Group one, Brainbox would work out the answers to the B test, scribble them on little bits of paper and pass them over to her. Brainbox had plenty of time for that sort of thing in tests. He always had his own test finished within twenty minutes.

However, Lizzie couldn't really be friends with Brainbox, Ace and His Nibs. She had one terrible disadvantage: she wasn't allowed to do anything at all. She always had to go home the quickest way after school. 'It takes ten minutes to get back,' Lizzie's mother claimed. She had timed it. If Lizzie wasn't home until fifteen minutes after school ended, she would see a careworn expression on her mother's face. If Lizzie didn't come rushing in until twenty minutes after school, her mother would be down at the main door of the apartment building weeping and wailing. What it would be like if she was ever a whole half hour late, Lizzie hardly dared to think.

'She'd probably call the police,' said Lizzie, 'if she hadn't had a heart attack first.'

Lizzie's mother was not nasty; she was just a terrible worrier. She was always worrying about Lizzie getting run over by a tram or falling under the wheels of a car. She worried even more about child molesters and sex murderers. When there was anything in the papers about cases of molestation and sexual attacks, as there often was, Lizzie's mother would beg her to try and get home in eight minutes. 'To set my mind at rest, Lizzie darling,' she said.

Lizzie couldn't go out alone in the afternoons, either. And her mother came to fetch her from afternoon gymnastics at school in winter, when it got dark early. Lizzie's mother would be waiting outside the school gates after choir practice, too. When Lizzie went swimming, her mother sat in the swimming baths building reading the paper, and when Lizzie went skating her mother sat beside the rink and watched.

You're bound to feel sorry for a girl as sheltered and protected as Lizzie, thought Brainbox, His Nibs and Ace. You can like her a lot, too. But you can't, they all agreed, be real friends with her, because you have to invest some of your free time in a real friendship, and Lizzie didn't have any. (All the same, Thomas Huber would have liked to be real friends with Lizzie. He'd fallen in love with her outside the school gates on the first day of term. Thomas Huber was so much in love, he'd have spent afternoons on end in Lizzie's apartment playing cards or dominoes with her and letting her mother stuff him with cake, even though he didn't like cards or dominoes, or cake either. But Lizzie did not return his love. Anyone who was enemies with His Nibs, Ace and Brainbox was an enemy of hers too. Thomas Huber could send her all the love letters he liked; it made no difference.)

Chapter 2

which introduces the reader to the eventful daily round of Ace, Nibs, Brainbox, Lizzie and the rest of Class 3D, and in which we get the first faint inkling of something very wrong.

There were fifteen double desks in 3D's classroom. Ten chairs and thus ten half-desks were empty. It was the 'flu season. Martina Mader, sitting at the back by the window, sneezed. Frau Meier, standing up in front by the board, said, 'Put your hand in front of your mouth, Martina, or you'll give the people next to you your germs.'

Martina Mader resentfully indicated the empty chair next to hers. 'Egon Schneider's got 'flu already. He gave me *his* germs.'

'Is that any reason to sneeze down my neck?' asked Thomas Huber, who sat in front of Martina, turning round and wiping the back of his neck.

'I *did* put my hand in front of my mouth,' said Martina.

She made a face, put both hands in front of her nose, and sneezed. Tiny but plentiful drops of spray escaped through her fingers.

'You did it again!' said Thomas Huber crossly, scrubbing at his cheeks with both hands.

'Thomas, come and wash your face!' said Frau Meier. Muttering crossly, Thomas Huber went over to the wash basin by the board.

Lizzie put her hand up. 'Please, Frau Meier, the tap's missing,' she pointed out.

Frau Meier looked at the wash basin and saw that the tap was indeed missing, or at least the handle of it, so that you couldn't turn it on. 'All right, go and wash in the cloakroom,

9

Thomas,' she said. Thomas was on his way to the door when Ace called, 'Hang on. I can fix it!'

Thomas stayed where he was. Ace went over to the wash basin, produced a pair of pliers from his trouser pocket, grasped the tap minus its handle with the pliers, and turned it. A thin stream of water ran into the basin.

'*At* your service, sir,' said Ace, bowing like a particularly polite head waiter serving champagne. 'Thanks, silly old Ass!' said Thomas Huber. He went over to the basin, let water run over his hands, splashed his face with it and spluttered. The class watched attentively. People in school always take a remarkable interest in anything that's not to do with lessons.

'That will do, Thomas,' said Frau Meier.

Thomas Huber turned away from the basin, shaking drops of water off his hands. Ace grasped the tap in his pliers again. 'Oh, bloody hell!' he said. He held up the pliers. The tap had come away in them. 'Stupid thing—it's broken!' he added. 'Now I can't turn the water off at all!'

Robert Sedlak, in the front row, put his hand up. 'Please, Frau Meier, shall I go and fetch the caretaker?'

Thomas Huber, half way back to his desk, also volunteered. 'Please, Frau Meier, wouldn't it be better if I go and get Herr Meznik? He could mend it better, and he wouldn't be so cross.'

'No one is going to fetch anybody!' said Frau Meier impatiently. She looked at the time. 'We've wasted quite enough of this lesson already! Let the water go on running, and you can fetch the caretaker at break.'

She turned back to the blackboard. It had words on it, in Latin. *Laudo, laudas, laudat.*

Thomas Huber went back to his desk. Ace hesitated, and then said, 'Please, Frau Meier, don't you think I ought to go and fetch somebody to do something, because—'

'No, I don't think you ought to do anything of the kind!'
Frau Meier interrupted him.

'But please, you see the water—'

'Otto Elterlein, will you kindly stop going on about the water? I know you! I'm not falling for any more of your ideas for enlivening the Latin lesson!' Frau Meier handed Ace a piece of chalk. 'Put your mind to something more sensible.' She pointed to the board. 'Finish conjugating that verb!'

Hesitantly, Ace took the chalk, but he kept looking at the wash basin in a worried kind of way.

'Well, Otto?' said Frau Meier. '*Laudo, laudas, laudat*—how does it go on?'

'But please, the water—' said Ace.

'Never mind about the water,' Frau Meier interrupted. She was already pretty cross; you could tell because there was a short but deep line between her eyebrows. This line could elongate itself at amazing speed until it reached her hairline, and once it reached her hairline you were in for one of her outbreaks of fury, and that meant extra homework, lots of it. Ace looked anxiously at the line between Frau Meier's eyebrows, and wrote, *Laudamus: we praise* on the board.

'Good, Otto. Now, *you praise.*'

Laudatis: you praise, wrote Ace, and there was very little of the line between Frau Meier's eyebrows left. Then Ace wrote, *Laudant: they praise*, and the skin of Frau Meier's forehead was smooth as a baby's bottom again. However, this happy state of affairs lasted only a minute, because then Martina Mader sneezed violently again, and Thomas Huber cried, 'Honestly, she's drenching me!'

'I can't *help* it,' said Martina, in a hoarse and weepy voice. Two yellowish drips were hanging from her nose.

'Blow your nose, Martina!' said Frau Meier.

'I haven't got a hanky,' said Martina, wiping her nose on

the sleeve of her blouse.

'Who can lend Martina a handkerchief?' asked Frau Meier. The little line was back between her eyebrows. Everyone began murmuring and pushing things about, searching satchels, going through the contents of trouser pockets. 'Lost mine,' people were saying, and, 'Used them all myself.'

The line between Frau Meier's eyebrows was climbing towards her hairline. Frau Meier went to the teacher's desk and took a tissue out of her handbag. She held it out, waiting for Martina to come and get it, but Martina stayed put.

'I don't think she's feeling well,' said Susi Kratochwil.

Frau Meier went over to Martina's desk and put a hand on her forehead. 'You've got a temperature,' she said, 'you ought to be in bed.'

'She had a temperature yesterday,' said Johanna Dohnal.

'Then what on earth are you doing here, child? Really, how silly!' Frau Meier shook her head. Martina sneezed, took the tissue, blew her nose and sneezed again. 'Because it's tests next week,' she sniffed, between sneezes. 'So I won't miss anything, my mum said.' There were three extremely noisy, wet sneezes, and then Martina moaned, 'So I won't get bad marks.'

'Thomas,' said Frau Meier, sighing, 'take Martina to the office and tell them to ring her home and ask someone to come and fetch her! And help her pack her satchel, Thomas. She's in no state to do it herself!'

Thomas Huber did not look particularly pleased. Reluctantly, he put his hand inside Martina's desk. 'Yuk!' he cried, snatching it back. He had touched a pile of sopping wet, crumpled paper tissues. The tissues fell out of the desk, like lots of little white paper dumplings. 'Am I supposed to pick them up, or what?' whined Thomas, crossly.

Frau Meier looked helplessly at the germ-sodden white dumplings on the floor. Then His Nibs stood up, went over to the waste paper basket, picked it up, took it over to Martina's desk, crouched down and shovelled the white dumplings into it with both hands. 'Used tissues don't actually kill, you know,' he murmured.

'Thank you, Michael, that's very kind of you,' said Frau Meier. She took Martina's satchel out of her desk, stuffed everything on top of the desk into the satchel, and handed it to Thomas. Martina rose unsteadily to her feet and sneezed again. Thomas made a disgusted face, but he took Martina's arm and led her out of the classroom. Frau Meier waited until the door had closed behind the two of them, and then said, 'Very well, now let's get on with the lesson!' She walked back to the front of the class, up to the board, and as she reached the wash basin her eyes widened in surprise. The wash basin was full to the brim, and more water kept flowing happily in from the connection without any tap or handle. 'For heaven's sake, it's overflowing!' cried Frau Meier. Her voice was shrill, and there were three lines on her forehead, two vertical and one horizontal.

Ace spoke up. 'Please, I *did* want to fetch the caretaker!'

'Well, run along and fetch him, then, and quick!'

Ace set off. But not quick enough, evidently, for Frau Meier screeched after him, 'And kindly *hurry*! This is no time for sleepwalking!' Then Frau Meier stared at the basin, obviously hoping that in the last resort the water might rise up into a mountain.

Brainbox, sitting in the front row, took his thumb out of his mouth. 'There's more running in than can run out, you see. Because the S-bend's blocked up,' he said.

'Has been for ages,' added Ferdi Berger.

'Then why didn't anyone say so? Why are you all sitting there like dummies waiting for it to overflow? Are you all crazy?' By now Frau Meier's forehead was positively criss-crossed with lines going both ways. She was quivering, whether with rage or desperation it was hard to tell. 'Where's a bowl?' Frau Meier looked round her. 'We must bale it out! Come along, someone bale it out!'

Hesitantly, Regine Habersack picked up the tiny flower vase she had on her desk. The vase was no bigger than a liqueur glass.

'Never mind the silly jokes, Regine!' spat Frau Meier. 'It's going to run over!'

His Nibs put his head on one side, closed one eye, squinted at the basin with the other, and remarked, 'Three more millimetres and it'll reach highwater-mark.'

'No, it's got at least five millimetres to go,' Lizzie contradicted him.

'Somebody get a bowl and bale it out!' wailed Frau Meier.

'Please, we haven't *got* a bowl,' said Lizzie. 'And none of the other classes would have one either. Only flower vases. And please, they're full of water already!'

'There must be an old saucepan or something *somewhere* in this wretched building!' screeched Frau Meier.

Brainbox rose to his feet and strolled slowly over to the wash basin. He opened a small metal door in the wall under the basin and turned something behind it. The water stopped running. 'The stopcock,' said Brainbox, mildly.

Frau Meier tottered over to the chair at the teacher's desk and sank into it.

The water-level in the basin was slowly going down, but Frau Meier's forehead was as criss-crossed with lines as ever.

'Daniel,' she inquired, in a trembling voice, 'did you know how to turn the water off all the time?'

Brainbox nodded. 'I was only waiting to see if anyone else would think of it,' he said.

Frau Meier took a deep breath in order to deliver a lengthy speech, and judging by her criss-crossed forehead it would have been a pretty blistering one, when the classroom door opened and Ace came in with the caretaker.

'What's the trouble this time?' asked the caretaker.

'The trouble *was* an overflowing basin!' said Frau Meier. 'But it's all right,' she added, proudly, pointing to the wash basin. 'We turned it off at the stopcock, and the danger's over.'

Herr Stribany the caretaker was the worst-tempered school caretaker in the city. He looked at Frau Meier nastily and said, 'So you chase me up out of my tea-break to tell me it's all right and you don't need me?'

'Well, you see, it *wasn't* all right when I sent for you, Herr Stribany,' said Frau Meier, apologetically. 'We've only just found out—'

'I know, I know!' Herr Stribany interrupted. 'Always scream for the caretaker first, that's the way it is! Simpler than using your own wits!' He turned to the door, and as the bell began ringing for break at that moment no one could quite make out his parting shot. Opinion differed as to whether it was something uncomplimentary about the state of the plumbing in the school buildings, or something equally uncomplimentary about Frau Meier.

After the last of the water had gurgled away down the plughole, and Frau Meier herself had left the classroom, looking cross, 3D sat back and congratulated themselves on a pleasant Latin lesson. 'She didn't even ask for our homework!' rejoiced Johanna Dohnal, hopping about the room on one leg.

'Didn't set any more homework either!' This made Ace so happy that he flung his arms around Thomas Huber, who had just come back into the classroom and who couldn't stand Ace, so that he took it as badly as he had just taken

Martina Mader's fits of sneezing.

Then the bell rang for the end of break. Next period was maths, and the maths master liked to find everyone sitting at their desks when he entered the room. It is better not to annoy such an important personage as a maths master, especially when it's tests next week, so 3D fell in with the maths master's wishes and sat down. And Ferdi Dalmar, who sat nearest the door, stood by it waiting to nod at the maths master and close the door behind him.

Brainbox moved his thumb to the corner of his mouth and muttered, to Lizzie, 'All this fuss and bother about that sergeant-major of a maths master!' Brainbox made some such remark before every maths lesson, and in the usual way Lizzie murmured agreement. This time Lizzie said nothing. She had her satchel on her lap and was searching it frantically.

'Looking for something?' asked Brainbox.

'I can't find my purse,' whispered Lizzie, and went on searching. She was still at it when the maths master marched into the classroom, and Ferdi bowed and scraped and shut the door behind him.

Everyone in the class jumped up and stood to attention, except Lizzie, who couldn't stand to attention because she was clutching her satchel.

'Sit down!' snapped the maths master. Worn out with all this military drill, 3D sank into its chairs. As she sat down, Lizzie dropped her satchel. All sorts of school things fell out, also stuff that had nothing to do with school. Lizzie bent down to salvage her possessions.

'What on earth are you doing?' asked the maths master.

'I dropped my satchel,' said Lizzie.

'You'd think anybody would have noticed that,' murmured Brainbox.

'Why don't you keep it in your desk?' asked the maths

master. 'Then you *couldn't* drop it.'

'I was looking for my purse,' Lizzie explained. 'I've lost my money!'

'What *do* you mean?' The maths master looked at Lizzie sternly, put his hands in his trouser pockets and marched up to her.

'My purse was still in my satchel before Latin,' said Lizzie. 'Really it was—I saw it. And now it's gone. Honestly!'

The maths master took one hand out of his trouser pocket, and swept the arm it belonged to around the classroom. 'So you are accusing one of your fellow pupils of theft?'

'No, I'm not!' cried Lizzie, shaking her head and going red in the face.

'Are you quite sure this purse of yours was in your satchel?' The maths master bent over Lizzie. 'Absolutely sure? One hundred per cent?'

. 'You might have left it at home,' Ace whispered, from the desk behind her.

'Easy to make a mistake like that,' murmured Brainbox.

'How much was there in it?' asked His Nibs quietly.

'Well?' The maths master rocked on the tips of his toes and looked hard at Lizzie.

Lizzie looked helpless. 'Oh, I don't know!' she said, and she put her satchel in her desk and sat down.

'Very sensible of you, Lizzie. Accusations of theft are not to be made lightly.' The maths master went back to the teacher's desk, opened the register and said, 'Anyone come in late or go home early?'

'Please, Martina Mader went home because she was sneezing so much,' said Oliver Schmied, standing in for the class spokesman, Michael Hanak, who was away, sick.

The maths master entered Martina Mader absent in the register, and Brainbox told Lizzie, comfortingly, 'Bet your

17

purse is at home.'

'Same thing happened to me once, Lizzie,' said Ace. 'I could have sworn I'd got my tram pass in my pocket, and it was in my desk the whole time!'

'Sure,' said His Nibs. 'I mean, there aren't any thieves in this class.'

The maths master snapped the register shut and called, 'Silence, please! The matter has been cleared up!'

Chapter 3

in which more people in 3D lose things, and morale sinks very low, and suspicion spreads like wildfire.

However, 'the matter' had not by any means been 'cleared up' as simply as the maths master supposed. Or not for Lizzie, anyway, because of Lizzie's mother being such a terrible worrier. And worriers tend to hit the ceiling if something isn't the way it ought to be: if something is mysterious, muddled, suspicious and hard to explain. Lizzie's mother hit the ceiling very hard indeed over that lost purse. Not because of the money, or the purse itself. What horrified Lizzie's mother was to think there was a sneaky, spiteful thief lurking somewhere near Lizzie. And it was only a step, she said to herself, from being a sneakthief to being an outright robber, and only another step from there to being a murderer, depending on the circumstances of the crime. For instance, the thief just had to give away his identity, and Lizzie, his victim, just had to let out a scream, and he would be hitting poor Lizzie over the head, and Lizzie would fall over and crack her skull on the paved surface of the road or somewhere, and the poor innocent child would be dead! It was only with great difficulty that Lizzie's mother could be dissuaded from fetching her from school in the middle of a bright and sunny day. Lizzie fought bravely, and desperately, against the prospect of this maternal escort. 'Don't you dare come and stand outside school at lunchtime!' she said. 'Don't you *dare*! If you do I'll go down to the boiler room and lock myself in and I'll never come out again! I'd rather spend all night in the boiler room than have you taking me home like a little kid in nursery class!'

It worked. Lizzie's mother sighed heavily, and lamented the fact that her poor child had no sense at all and was going to be delivered up to the powers of evil of her own pigheaded free will, but she said no more about fetching her from school. Lizzie's mother was also very angry with the maths master, who had simply ignored the theft of the purse. Lizzie's mother knew very well that her daughter didn't go losing purses on the way to school! If her daughter said the purse had been in her satchel at break, then it *had* been there at break! Lizzie's mother went over the whole thing again seven times daily.

It got on Lizzie's father's nerves. 'Well, why don't you go up to school and tell them what you think?' he said impatiently. 'And make them call the police in to find the thief!'

'Good heavens, Ottokar, what an idea!' said Lizzie's mother, horrified. 'I'm certainly not going up to school to get into an argument with the teachers! That sort of thing only does your own child harm!'

Lizzie's father sighed, and said he thought there were other ways of doing your own child harm, too.

'And what's that supposed to mean, Ottokar?' asked Lizzie's mother, voice rising, but Lizzie's father just sighed again, twice, and said nothing. He had given up arguing with his wife about the rearing and over-protection of children long ago.

There was much discussion of the lost purse at Lizzie's home, but none at all at school. Lizzie didn't mention it again; she had quite enough of her mother going on and on about that purse at home. So Brainbox, Ace, His Nibs and the others thought it must have turned up again.

A week of perfectly normal school with its perfectly normal irritations went by in a perfectly normal way. Brainbox provided Lizzie with the answers to all four of her maths questions in the test, as usual, and he scribbled the answers on little bits of paper and passed them back to Ace and His Nibs as well, two each. The caretaker fitted a new tap to the classroom wash basin. The people who had been away with 'flu came back to school one by one. And during break 3D wandered up and down the rows of desks muttering beautiful lines of poetry such as, 'The old man struck his harp strings, he struck them wondrous loud,' or 'For in his mind is horror, and in his eyes is rage; his voice a scourge, he writes his words in blood upon the page.'

The reason for this was that they had to learn Ludwig Uhland's poem *The Minstrel's Curse* by heart for German, and as the poem has sixteen great long verses, and 3D were having trouble getting those sixteen verses into their heads, they all wore deep frowns as they wandered up and down the rows of desks reciting poetry.

It was particularly hard for His Nibs. He was never much good at learning by heart, and there was just no way he could remember things like, 'And so the youth expired.'

'Expired, expired, oh, blast it and bother it, expired!' wailed His Nibs. 'I *will* rember the stupid word, I *will*!' But a moment later he had to open his German book again to look up the peculiar word the poet Uhland had used for dying.

And then, on Monday in fourth break, something happened. Fourth break was just before the German lesson when they were going to be tested on *The Minstrel's Curse*. His Nibs was sitting cross-legged on the teacher's desk, saying crossly, 'Woe to thee, wicked murderer, thou bane of minstrelsy! In vain may all thy laurels for bloodstained striving be!'

Lizzie, who was standing beside him, shook her head. 'No, Nibs, it's *striving* for bloodstained *laurels*.'

'Comes to the same thing anyway, doesn't it?' groaned His Nibs, running the fingers of one hand through his black curls and picking his elegant nose with the forefinger of the other hand. 'Can't make head or tail of it. Clear as mud.'

Lizzie was just going to say that anyone who was always being held up to the class as a fine example of the correct use of their native tongue ought to be able to get the hang of an easy little verse of a ballad, when Martina Mader suddenly let out a screech. 'I don't believe it! It isn't true!'

She was standing beside her desk holding a small blue box. The box was empty. Martina, stunned, was staring at the empty box. It was the box for the milk money. Every Monday morning, before the first bell went, Martina collected the money from everyone who wanted school milk in the ten o'clock break, and she put it in this small blue box, to be given to the caretaker after school. She had already collected milk money from all the milk drinkers today except one, His Nibs. And she had just been going over to His Nibs to ask for his milk money, so she picked up the blue box, fully expecting to lift quarter of a kilo of Austrian schillings inside it—and she found nothing but ten grams of empty box in her hand.

'The money's all gone!' cried Martina.

The people who had been wandering about reciting poetry stopped dead in their tracks. *The Minstrel's Curse* died away. They all looked at the empty blue box, just as stunned as Martina had been a moment ago, but Martina was looking round the room in search of someone. She found him: Ferdi Berger. Ferdi was beside the waste paper basket with his German book and a half-peeled orange in one hand, and several bits of orange peel in the other.

'Is this another of your silly jokes, Ferdi?' inquired Martina.   Ferdi Berger was a joker. As such, he was the terror of 3D. He either told long shaggy dog stories from beginning to end, having first given away the point of the joke and asked if anyone knew it. If you told him you'd known that story ever since nursery school, he was delight-

22

ed, and told it all the same. Or else he did things he thought immensely funny. He put super-glue on the seat of Michi Hanak's chair. He swapped round everyone's plimsolls in their shoe-bags. He put a live worm in Lizzie's packet of sandwiches for break. He offered people sweets with salt in them, and sewed up the sleeves of their jackets. Nobody in the class thought Ferdi's long and involved stories or his peculiar practical jokes at all funny, but Ferdi didn't mind. Undeterred, he came up with a new joke daily.

'You stupid idiot, Ferdi!' said Martina furiously, marching up to him. 'If you've gone and taken the milk money for a joke you can just give it back, or I'll thump you so hard you won't know your own name!' And to lend substance to this threat, Martina raised her right arm in a ready-to-thump position.

Ferdi dropped his orange peel in alarm. 'It wasn't me!' he stammered. '*I* haven't got your milk money! Honest!'

'Honest?' Martina's right arm was still raised.

'Yes, honest, Martina!' Ferdi assured her. 'I promise I didn't take it. I mean, that *would* have been a silly joke!'

'That's what he said when he hid my gym shoes,' said Susi Kratochwil. 'He promised he hadn't taken *them*, but he had, all the same!' Susi Kratochwil was small and plump with a vast quantity of curly hair the same colour as a goldfish. She was very proud of it. She and Ferdi had been sworn enemies for over ten years. Their enmity dated back to a quarrel in the sandpit, when Susi had thrown sand into Ferdi's face, took in the bite Ferdi had inflicted on Susi at primary school, and at the latest count included the knockout blow Susi had delivered to Ferdi on the occasion of the hidden gym shoes.

'Look, hiding a pair of gym shoes isn't the same as stealing the milk money!' protested Ferdi. 'I don't play practical jokes with money. Wouldn't touch it! I'm not that sort!'

Martina let her arm sink. She felt sure Ferdi was telling

the truth. Not because she thought he was a particularly honest boy, but because she knew exactly what Ferdi looked like when he was lying. He wore a silly, embarrassed sort of grin when he was lying, and at the moment he was looking perfectly serious.

His Nibs got off the teacher's desk and went over to the waste paper basket, Ferdi and Martina, along with Lizzie. Ferdi and Martina were already surrounded by the rest of the class.

'When did the milk money disappear?' His Nibs asked.

'I've no idea.' Martina shrugged her shoulders. 'I collected the money first thing and put the lid on the box. I haven't looked inside it since. I mean, I was sure the money *was* in there until just now. But of course it could have gone ages ago.'

'How about the gym lesson?' asked His Nibs. 'Did you leave the box on your desk then?'

Martina nodded, gloomily.

'Then someone must have come and taken the money during gym,' said Ace. He patted Martina's shoulder encouragingly and added, 'Nothing you can do about it. We'll just have to pay a second lot of milk money. It isn't all that much.'

'Oh, *will* we, though?' said Thomas Huber indignantly. 'Why should I have to pay twice? *I'm* not such an ass as that!' He tapped his forehead. 'The thief will have to give the money back!'

Ace grinned. 'That's it, Thomas, you write a note and put it up on the notice board. Wanted: honest thief to return our milk money!'

A few people giggled, and Thomas Huber's ears went red, which was a sign that he was very cross. 'You silly Ass,' he hissed at Ace, 'it's no laughing matter, people stealing things in school!'

24

Ace explained that he wasn't laughing at the money being stolen, he was laughing at Thomas Huber for being so stupid. Thomas Huber's ears went redder than ever, positively ruby-red, and he thrust his head forward like a bull about to go for a bullfighter, and he certainly *would* have gone for Ace if Dr Hufnagel hadn't happened to come into the classroom at that moment.

'Hullo, what's going on? Something wrong?' asked Dr Hufnagel. She was 3D's form mistress, and she was one of the sensitive sort of teachers who notice at once if a class is upset or excited.

'That Ass keeps making fun of me! The whole time!' shouted Thomas Huber, and the others had to point out to him that this was merely a side issue, nothing to do with the real trouble, and not worth mentioning any more.

'Now then, children, go back to your desks first, please,' said Dr Hufnagel. 'And then one of you can tell me what's happened. If you all talk at once I can't make out a word you say.'

The gathering around the waste paper basket dispersed. Martina waited until they were all back at their desks, and then she told Dr Hufnagel about the missing milk money. Dr Hufnagel suggested searching for the milk money. 'You might have put it somewhere else, Martina,' she said. 'Or it could have fallen out of the box and rolled over the floor and it's lying in a corner somewhere.'

Martina protested vigorously. She said she wasn't the absent-minded sort who did things and then forgot about them. She'd been collecting the milk money for three years, and she'd never put it anywhere except the box, she'd always taken it straight to the caretaker in its box, and how could coins fall out of the box if the lid didn't come off the box first?

Dr Hufnagel saw that she had a point there. She looked

sad. And then she made a long and sorrowful speech about children who do not respect the property of others, and expressed a heartfelt wish that they would leave no money or valuables lying about if they had to go out of the classroom. 'It is a shame, and very unfortunate, children,' she said, 'but in a large school like this I'm afraid there are always a few people who will behave badly. I don't see any prospect of finding the thief. It would be a remarkable coincidence if we did! The only way of guarding against theft, my dears, is to make sure we don't leave things lying around!' And then Dr Hufnagel sighed, and said they had discussed this sad business enough now and they had better remember this was the German lesson. She asked Michi Hanak to recite the first verse of *The Ministrel's Curse*.

While Michi Hanak was droning out the information that in times of ancient story there stood a castle high, and over all the country it shone 'twixt earth and sky, Brainbox leaned over to Lizzie, took his thumb out of his mouth and whispered, 'So we're in the gym, someone from another class says he's got to go to the cloakroom, he leaves his classroom, he comes into our classroom, he makes straight for Martina's desk, he takes the milk money out of the box and he makes off again. Do *you* think that's what happened?'

Lizzie shook her head.

'I don't, either,' muttered Brainbox.

'What *do* you think, then?' Lizzie whispered.

But Brainbox couldn't tell her, because he was called upon to recite the second verse of the poem.

German was the last lesson that Monday, and when the bell rang at the end of it 3D were worn out by the minstrel's curse. A whole period jabbering ballads and having ballads jabbered back really takes it out of you. Exhausted, they all packed up their school books and went down to the cloak-rooms in the basement. Nobody said anything much about the milk money. They were discussing afternoon games, in three hours' time, and His Nibs and Ace, the two best handball players in the class, were saying they simply didn't feel up to handball, considering the awful time they'd had with that minstrel and his curse.

'We shall lose miserably,' Ace prophesied, and he yawned.

'Go home and have a rest,' suggested Michi Hanak, and Ace said he couldn't have a rest, because he had a baby sister who *had* to have a rest at mid-day and didn't want to, so she kept chattering at the top of her voice, keeping other people awake.

'Try earplugs,' said Brainbox. 'They help. My mother can't sleep without earplugs. They soundproof you.' Brainbox put his indoor shoes in his locker and started looking for his outdoor shoes. 3D's cloakroom was usually very untidy. The children called it the monkey cage, and that was just what it looked like. Each class had a monkey cage of its own down in the basement of the school building: a square, barred area with two benches in it, hooks to hang coats on, and a door that could be locked. The caretaker unlocked the doors at quarter to eight in the morning. He locked them again on the dot of eight, when the bell went, and if anyone wanted to get into one of the monkey cages during lessons or in break he had to fetch the key from the caretaker. And at the end of school, when the children wanted to get back into the cloakrooms to change, somebody had to go and fetch the key of the monkey cage from the caretaker too. This strict system of locking and unlocking had been introduced a few years before, when all sorts of things kept disappearing from the unlocked cloakrooms. Since then the monkey cages were supposed to be absolutly burglar-proof. If Brainbox hadn't known that he would have sworn somebody had pinched his outdoor shoes, because they were nowhere to be

27

seen. However, he did finally discover his right shoe behind the open cage door, and he dug the left shoe out of a mountain of shoes in the middle of the cage. 'Yuk!' grumbled Brainbox, rummaging through the mountain of shoes. 'Somebody's got sweaty feet! This lot stink like a cheese counter!' And Brainbox glanced up and looked around, wondering which of his dear friends to accuse of sweaty feet. His eyes fell on Rosalind Fröhlich. Rosalind was sitting on the cloakroom bench in front of him, with tears in her eyes.

'Hullo, Rosalind, what's up?' said Brainbox. 'I mean, it's nothing to cry about! Don't be silly! Just a stupid old poem, that's all!' Brainbox thought Rosalind was crying over *The Minstrel's Curse.*

She had had to recite three times during German, and she hadn't been able to say a single line correctly on any of those three occasions. So Dr Hufnagel had marked her work 'Unsatisfactory' in the little red marks book.

'Unsatisfactory doesn't mean a thing, not in oral work,' said Brainbox, trying to comfort Rosalind. 'And you're pretty good at written tests, aren't you?'

Rosalind Fröhlich shook her head, and a big tear trickled out of each eye and rolled down her cheeks. Brainbox found a handkerchief in his trouser pocket and offered it to her. Rosalind took the handkerchief, blew her nose, and said, 'Who cares about silly old Hufnagel and her Unsatisfactory? I've lost my fifty Austrian schillings. All my pocket money. I found my purse under the bench, open and empty. They even took my tram tickets.'

'Honest?' asked Brainbox. Rosalind nodded. She showed him her empty purse and told him she'd left it in her coat pocket that morning.

'Hey, come and listen to this, everyone!' called Brainbox. 'Rosalind's lost *her* money too!'

About half of 3D were still in the cloakroom, but at this

they made more noise than seven complete classes put together. There were shouts of, 'She hasn't, has she?' and, 'Can't be true!' And, 'Maybe it fell out of her pocket!' And, 'Let's look under the benches!'

His Nibs and Brainbox crawled around the floor, feeling behind the benches and getting filthy knees and dirty hands. Wolfgang Hahn hit his head on the doorframe in the course of the search. Martina Mader went round shaking out coats and jackets. Ace shook the bar with the coathooks on it. Rosalind got an attack of sneezing from all the dust, and Lizzie got a splinter in her thumb. But they didn't find the fifty schillings.

'Oh no!' said Ace gloomily, when they had called off the search. 'Someone in our class *must* be the thief. Nobody else comes into this monkey cage!'

'But the caretaker has the key,' said His Nibs.

'So?' Lizzie shook her head. 'You don't mean you think Herr Stribany—'

'Oh, don't be silly,' said His Nibs, indignantly, interrupting her. 'But someone could have stolen the key from him!'

'I just fetched it from him myself, though!' said Michi Hanak. 'It was hanging on the board—it hadn't been stolen!'

His Nibs still wasn't giving up the idea. 'It could have been put back again, on the quiet!'

Lizzie shook her head. 'Rubbish,' she said. 'Nibs, your ideas are always so far-fetched! You dream up the most complicated explanations for the simplest things!'

'Okay, and how does *your* simple explanation go?' asked His Nibs, looking bad-tempered.

'*My* simple explanation,' said Lizzie, 'is there's someone in our class stealing things like a magpie. First my purse, then the milk money, now Rosalind's fifty schillings. He must be rolling in it!'

'Why *he*?' asked Brainbox, without taking his thumb out of his mouth. 'Could be a girl. Or don't you think girls ever steal things?'

Lizzie shrugged her shoulders. 'Look, I've got to go home now or Mum will blow her top,' she said. She gave her indoor shoes a kick, and they landed in a corner of the monkey cage.

The others picked up their satchels and left the cloakroom with Lizzie. Michi Hanak closed the cloakroom door, and they climbed up the basement steps in silence. Herr Stribany was standing at the top of the steps, holding out his hand. Michi Hanak gave him the cloakroom key. 'Hurry up, can't you?' growled the caretaker. 'If I had to stand about waiting for all the cloakroom keys this long I'd wear my legs out!'

'Please, Herr Stribany,' asked His Nibs, 'did anybody come and get our cloakroom key for any special reason today?'

The caretaker looked impatiently at His Nibs. 'When would they have done that?' His Nibs shrugged his shoulders, and the caretaker asked, 'Which class are you, anyway?'

'Tells you on the key tag,' murmured Brainbox.

'3D, please,' said His Nibs.

'Class with the tap that went wrong?' The caretaker was now looking very cross indeed. His Nibs nodded. 'Nothing but trouble with you lot!' snapped the caretaker. 'And no, nobody came for your key today!'

'Are you sure?' asked Brainbox.

'Well, for heaven's sake, what's the idea of all these stupid questions?' The caretaker went red in the face with fury. 'Standing there talking nonsense! Nobody came for any key at all today, so nobody can have come for your key, right?' And the caretaker turned and shuffled off, muttering morosely to himself.

'Might as well go too,' said Ace. 'There's nothing we can do about it now.' And 3D walked slowly towards the school gates, headed by Lizzie, who was in more of a hurry than the rest. Once she reached the gates she waved to the others and dashed off. She was eight minutes late already, which meant sixteen minutes of maternal reproaches.

Martina caught up with Lizzie at the corner of the school building. 'You know what I think?' she said, panting. 'I think Rosalind just wants to look important. She always loves being in the limelight! She's lying, that's what it is. Somebody stole my milk money, so now she says *she's* lost something too.'

'I don't think that's it,' said Lizzie.

'But she hid her own gym things last year, remember?'

'Only because she didn't want to do gym,' said Lizzie.

'Rubbish!' Martina's voice was venomous. 'It was because she likes people to make a fuss of her. She's a show-off, I tell you! She just stood by and watched when people thought Babsi Binder had stolen her things! Just let them suspect her!'

'Look, that's not true!' Lizzie stopped. 'You're only saying so because you don't like Rosalind. When she realized people suspected Babsi she admitted she'd hidden her gym things right away!'

'Only because she had to! Because Ferdi Dalmar had *seen* her hiding them!' And Martina tapped her forehead. 'Honestly, Lizzie, you're so naive! You've no idea the way things *really* are!'

They had reached the point where Lizzie had to turn left and Martina right.

'Like me to come a bit farther with you?' asked Martina.

'No, thanks, I'm in a hurry.' And Lizzie ran across the road while the lights were green. She was glad to get away from Martina. She's really mean, thought Lizzie. Mean and nasty. Always knows something horrid about other people. But then, as Lizzie was walking down the street to the building where she lived, she thought: perhaps there *is* something in what she says! Rosalind's a bit odd. If you say you went to the pictures at the weekend, she says she went to the pictures too. If you say you're getting a new record player for your birthday, she says she's getting one too. It just *could* be she wants to have had something stolen from her because another person did.

Lizzie sighed deeply as she reached the door of the apartment building. Whether because of her worrying thoughts about Rosalind, or because of her careworn, frowning mother, standing waiting in the doorway and looking reproachfully at her watch, it's hard to say.

Chapter 4

in which, in the interests of realism, we print original extracts from Brainbox's diary.

Brainbox had been keeping a diary for several years. He didn't keep it in pretty little velvet-covered albums with flowery decorations and silly tinny locks making out they were top secret. Brainbox put his thoughts down on squared paper in blue A5 loose-leaf notebooks. He did not have to keep his thoughts under lock and key either, for they were not in the least top secret, far from it. The only reason Brainbox filled page after page of squared paper was that he had all sorts of thoughts in his head which didn't interest anyone. Thoughts about justice, thoughts about death and dying, thoughts about the possible genetic cause of miserliness, thoughts about the existence of God, or life on other planets, thoughts about evil and political parties and stupidity and marks at school and life in general. Even his best friends, Ace and His Nibs, weren't all that keen to discuss such subjects with Brainbox. They would listen to him patiently and try not to show their boredom. It was no good Brainbox trying his ideas out on his mother, either. In fact, they horrified her. 'Good gracious, Daniel,' she cried, when Brainbox began discussing them, 'a boy of your age shouldn't be thinking so hard! Time enough for that when you're grown up. You ought to be enjoying your childhood!'

If Brainbox protested, defending his right to think as much as he wanted and explaining that you couldn't actually *stop* yourself thinking, sometimes you couldn't even help lying awake at night with your thoughts, his mother would sigh unhappily and say, 'Oh dear, you *are* in a poor

33

way, Daniel! And being a woman, I'm afraid I'm no use to you.' For Brainbox's mother considered thinking man's work. Her own father had told her so, over and over, until she believed it.

Brainbox's mother was very sorry for her Daniel, not having a man about the place to help him with his thinking. Sometimes she wondered whether she shouldn't get married again, to provide him with someone in the family who knew how to think. She even brought a man home now and then and introduced him to Brainbox. Brainbox couldn't stand any of these men. He didn't even try discussing his thoughts with them; whenever one of them came, he went straight to his room and played records so loud that the visitor's ears quivered, his head throbbed, and the sweat broke out on his forehead.

Whether this was why none of the men ever came visiting more than once is hard to say, but that was Brainbox's mother's opinion.

Of course Brainbox had a father too, one who apparently did a lot of thinking himself, but Brainbox was unable to find out whether this was actually true because his father lived in Switzerland. The divorce courts had given his father the right to see his son once a week and for two months in the summer, but his father didn't take advantage of that right, and as the divorce courts had said nothing about a son having the right to see his father, it was nearly nine years since the pair of them last met.

Brainbox never talked about his father. If anyone asked about his father he said, 'I haven't got one. Never did.' And if the other person persisted, saying everybody has to have a father, Brainbox said, 'Yes, sure. But mine died before I was born.' He had even told His Nibs and Ace this fairy-tale, although they knew perfectly well it wasn't true. They could actually remember seeing Brainbox's father when they were all at nursery school. But they had agreed not to dispute the point with Brainbox.

'If he says his father's dead, I expect he's got his reasons,' said Ace, and His Nibs agreed with him.

Even in the blue diaries, there wasn't a single thought about Brainbox's father. Other people's fathers never figured in them either. They contained nothing about the things that happened to Brainbox day in, day out. He thought those things were far too boring to record.

Or such was the case until November 7th. On November 6th, Brainbox wrote three pages to the effect that he didn't believe in inborn stupidity, and he was sure no child was destined from birth to get its work described as 'Unsatisfactory' seven times over in its school report, but then, on November 7th and on the first page of a new blue A5 notebook, you might have read the following:

7th November
This is getting worse and worse!

Now it's Ivan's little chain that's gone. A gold chain with a little gold Asterix pendant on it. Ivan took it off before gym, because Herr Huber doesn't let anyone do gym with a pendant round his neck. So Ivan put it in the left-hand back pocket of his jeans. There isn't any doubt about that. I saw him do it myself. I was standing next to him. And then we went into the gym.

After gym there was a bit of confusion in the changing-room, because Thomas Huber was having a fight with Ace. And it's a fact that some of the clothes rails nearly tipped over in the fighting and several shirts and pairs of trousers went flying, but Ivan's jeans weren't among them. I know. I'd gone off into the far corner, because I don't want anything to do with fighting. And Ivan's jeans were in the far corner too, hanging just where they ought to be. But when Herr Huber had blown his whistle and stopped the scuffling, and Ivan had changed, and was going to take his chain out of his pocket, it

35

wasn't there.

So the chain must have been stolen before the scuffle. Which means during the gym lesson, or even before the gym lesson. And when you come to think of it that means a whole lot more. Only I don't want to come to think of it. It's not the kind of thinking I enjoy. It really is not.

The whole class is busy wondering who the thief is. They're getting quite hysterical, and whispering suspicions of someone the whole time. They all suspect whoever they like least. (For instance, Susi Kratochwil suspects Ferdi Berger, and Ace suspects Thomas Huber.) And His Nibs insists somebody from 3A was the thief, because we have gym with the boys from 3A. But so far nothing at all has gone from 3A itself. If I point that out to His Nibs, he says yes, that's logical. But the thief from 3A is clever, he says, too clever to pinch things from his own class, so he's picked us as his victims. I call that a stupid sort of theory! Lizzie agrees with me. She says it's perfectly obvious the thief is in our class, and it has to be a boy because there weren't any girls in the changing-room where Ivan lost his Asterix pendant. But Ace says it doesn't have to be the same thief all the time, we could be having a kind of epidemic. Everyone stealing something from someone else! Lizzie's purse, Martina's milk money, Rosalind's fifty schillings, Ivan's chain—all stolen by different people? Sounds crazy, but it's possible!

And now I'm right in the middle of thoughts I don't enjoy a bit, so I think I'd rather stop writing. I'd rather not think at all than go watching my friends like a sneaky spy, trying to find out who's the thief.

I'll borrow a crossword puzzle from Mum. And solve it. Crossword puzzles stop you thinking!

Brainbox didn't write a word in his diary on November 8th, because his mother was cleaning the apartment. She had one of these big cleaning days regularly, once a month, when she pushed all the furniture into the middle of the rooms, rolled up the carpets and washed and polished the floors till they shone. It wasn't that Brainbox's mother made him help, and thus kept him from writing his diary. Heaven forbid! Brainbox's mother thought cleaning was woman's work. That was something else her father had told her. She didn't ask her son to do a thing, but somehow he wasn't comfortable at home on cleaning days, so he spent the afternoon of November 8th with Ace. When he got back in the evening the furniture was in its usual place again, but there was such a strong smell of cleaning stuff in the air that Brainbox felt unable to do anything more strenuous than reading comic strips.

And he had no time to write in his diary on November 9th, because he was making Susi Kratochwil a puppet out of big wooden beads, felt, string and paint. He was giving it to Susi for her birthday. Brainbox did not particularly like Susi Kratochwil: rather the opposite, if anything. But she had invited him to her birthday party on November 10th, and you can't very well turn up at a birthday party without a present.

The puppet turned out extremely well. Any toyshop would have given it pride of place in its window. Brainbox felt very sorry he had to give it away to Susi. He spent quite a while wondering whether to keep the puppet and give Susi a packet of three herbal soaps from his mother's store cupboard instead. But the herbal soap smelt horrible, and Susi was a very posh sort of girl. In the end generosity won the day, and Brainbox wrapped his puppet up, sighing, in pink tissue paper, tied a sky-blue bow round it, and wrote a card saying WITH LOVE TO SUSI ON HER 13TH BIRTHDAY.

And on November 10th, Susi's birthday party itself kept Brainbox from writing anything in his diary.

In fact, the next entry was dated November 11th.

11th November
There was all hell to pay in school today!

It started first thing, at eight o'clock. I was just wondering why Frau Kratochwil had come up to school with Susi. I mean, Frau Kratochwil isn't another of Lizzie's mother's sort! And then I saw her marching off to the staffroom, and I wondered why even more, because I knew she hadn't been asked to come and see the staff. So I asked Susi what her mother was doing up at school. She gave me a funny sort of look. 'You'll soon find out,' she said, in an even funnier sort of voice.

And I did find out, too. Dr Hufnagel came into the classroom first period instead of the maths master. In itself that'd have been a nice surprise, but it wasn't that the maths master was away sick or anything like that. It was because Dr Hufnagel's our form mistress, and she told us Frau Kratochwil had been to see her and was very angry indeed. Frau Kratochwil said one of Susi's savings books had gone missing after the party yesterday. And it was perfectly clear only one of the guests at the party could have stolen it! And if the savings book wasn't returned within twelve hours Frau Kratochwil was threatening to call the police in! Police—I ask you! What can the police do about it? There were nineteen children at the party. Only eleven of them were from our class. And there were lots of other people in the Kratochwils' huge great house. For instance, there were some women who are friends of Frau Kratochwil's. And anyway, the savings book has a codeword, and nobody could draw any money out of it at all without knowing the codeword! And they've told the savings bank the book's been stolen, so even if anyone did know the codeword they still couldn't draw any money out.

I'm furious with Frau Kratochwil. And her daughter! The fuss they make! Susi's mother marched straight out of school again, but Susi went around all day as if she were surrounded by criminals! Why did she have to go taking her three savings books out and boasting about them? Twenty thousand Austrian schillings in this one, thirteen thousand in that one, a hundred thousand saved up for her in the other one! Showing off like that—serves her right! If I'd known this was

38

going to happen I'd have given her the herbal soap after all and kept my beautiful puppet.

So now the eleven of us from 3D at the party are prime suspects! Just like Nibs says, it could just as well have been one of Frau Kratochwil's friends who stole the savings book. Stupid females! They kept fluttering about, never left us in peace for a moment! Of course they were all terribly well off, but that's got nothing to do with it. I mean, there was once a public prosecutor who pinched a bottle of vodka from a supermarket. I read about it in the paper.

But what I say is, it's none of my business. What I tell myself is, if you don't take money to school, and you don't wear pendants round your neck on gold chains, and you keep an eye on the milk money, and you don't go boasting of your three savings books or keeping fifty schillings in your coat pocket, you can't go wrong!

And so I can't go wrong, because I haven't got any money or any gold chains, let alone savings books. And I've always managed to get out of having to collect money for anything. And there's nothing to steal in my trouser pockets except three half-price tram tickets, and if anyone wants those, he's welcome!

Next day, November 12th, Brainbox wrote the following in his diary in red ballpoint pen, which he generally used only for particularly important thoughts, and something had happened to his beautiful, neat, tidy handwriting. It all scribbles and scrawls and practically illegible, as if he had been writing in a rage.

12th November
I've had just about enough of this! The caretaker found Susi's stupid savings book when he was sweeping out the basement. It was all dirty and tattered. He took it to the Headmaster, and the Headmaster summoned the eleven of us from 3D who'd been to the party. The eleven are Ace, Michi Hanak, Nibs, Wolfi Hahn, Thomas Huber, Egon Schneider, Martina Mader, Lizzie, Robert Sedlak, me and

39

Andreas Knopf.

So the Head said that proved it was one of us. Michi Hanak protested. Four of the other children at the party go to our school too, he said, only they're in different classes. They could have put the savings book in the basement. And three more of our own class came to the party later, as Lizzie told the Head. They hadn't actually been invited, they rang the bell and said they only wanted to know the numbers of the maths problems for homework because they'd lost the list of them. And then they stayed. Those three were Ferdi Dalmar, Heinzi Böck and Johanna Dohnal, and that's what they always do when they want to go to a party and they haven't been invited.

The Head said he was sick and tired of the whole wretched business, he couldn't make it out, and the police weren't going to do any more about it now the savings book had turned up and no damage had been done; policemen don't have time to bother with petty offences like that.

And then the Head said he hoped nothing else was going to be stolen in our class, because if anything was stolen there would be very serious consequences.

And finally he looked hard at all of us, one by one, as if he wanted to make sure he knew what hardened criminals looked like! It was horrible! I wish I could catch a nice illness, something lasting three months, so I wouldn't have to go to school. I do feel awful today, anyway. I didn't know I was so sensitive. But ever since that interview with the Head I've had a funny, churning sort of feeling in my stomach. Stronger nerves, that's what I need!

Brainbox didn't catch an illness lasting three months, but he did have a minor gastric infection. As his mother had had the same sort of infection a week before, his could hardly be put down to mental turmoil. It is possible, however, that had he been in a happier frame of mind Brainbox would have got through it without going to bed. As it was, he went to bed and stayed there for five days. He didn't get up except to go to the lavatory, and he passed the time with a stack of Disney comics, a book about nuclear fission and his diaries. He filled an entire sixty-page notebook in those five days, but he didn't waste a single one of his thoughts on the thefts at school. When His Nibs and Ace visited him in the afternoons, he told them not to talk about it.

November 19th was the first day Brainbox went back to school, and he wrote the following in his diary, in blue ink this time and in his neat and legible handwriting.

19th November
It looks as if that horrible series of thefts is over at last. Nothing else was stolen at school all the time I was sick in bed at home.

Of course, supposing I were somebody who didn't like me I could always say that meant Brainbox was the thief!

Sounds logical, doesn't it?

And anyone sitting next to Lizzie can easily get at her purse.

And I borrowed Martina's pencil sharpener at break that day the milk money was stolen. Martina wasn't at her desk, so I borrowed it without asking. I could easily have emptied the milk money box without anyone noticing! (Thank goodness nobody knows I borrowed that pencil sharpener.)

And I was right beside Ivan's jeans with the Asterix pendant in their pocket, all the time the scuffle was going on. I could easily have pinched the pendant. Everyone was watching the scuffle—they wouldn't have noticed a thing.

And I went to Susi's birthday party. I was standing there beside Susi when she was showing off her savings books. I even went back into the same room three times after that, because that's where the delicious salmon sandwiches were.

And I don't have much money! To be honest, I have almost no money at all, and a person without any money is easily tempted to take someone else's. Or so everyone thinks. That's why Martina thought of Ferdi Berger straight away. That's why Michi Hanak told me he thought Robert Sedlak must be the thief.

There's only one other person in the class besides Robert Sedlak and Ferdi Berger who never has any money. Me!

So everything fits really neatly. I could be the thief! I wonder if that's occurred to anyone else? I wonder if there's anyone who hates me so much they'd think of it? No, that's silly! You wouldn't have to hate me to think of it. I mean, I thought of it. And I quite like myself.

Chapter 5

in which the maths master starts something which has sensational consequences, deeply impressing the majority of 3D and casting the small minority of 3D into the utmost confusion and despair.

Class 3D went on in this pleasant, peaceful, theft-free way for over a week, until December 1st. But then, a few moments before long break ended on December 1st, Johanna Dohnal suddenly let out a screech. 'Oh no!' she screeched. 'I don't believe it! It isn't true! It *can't* be gone!' And Johanna Dohnal got down on the floor and went crawling about on all fours, with her face quite close to the floorboards, because she was rather short-sighted. Anyone could see she was looking for something. And everybody wanted to know just what she so badly wanted to find. But it was not until the earsplitting noise of the bell for the end of break had died away that they could make out what Johanna was wailing as she crawled about the floor. 'My watch!' she was wailing. 'My lovely new watch! It's gone! It was real gold, self-winding, on a gold bracelet, and now it's gone!' And Johanna Dohnal drummed both fists on the floorboards, shouting, 'I'll *murder* whoever took my watch, I'll murder him, I will! If somebody's stolen my watch I'll *murder* him!' Nobody could make out the rest of what she said, because she punctuated it with three very long, very loud sobs after each syllable.

'Oh no, oh, not again, oh, heaven help us!' muttered Brainbox, and then he did what everybody else was doing: he bent down and scrutinized the floorboards at his feet in search of Johanna Dohnal's gold watch. And like everybody else, he was thinking it was an utterly pointless exercise.

You'd spot a showy watch like that straight off, with its gold bracelet and all, thought Brainbox. It hasn't fallen on the floor or slipped behind anything. It's been stolen!

There was considerable confusion in the classroom, with thirty people searching pointlessly and helplessly for the watch. A couple of chairs fell over, several books and pencils slid to the floor, Michi Hanak trod on Martina Mader's hand and Martina shrieked like a stuck pig. Ace's elbow knocked Wolfgang Hahn's glasses off his nose. Wolfgang Hahn yelled, 'Watch out—my glasses! Where've they gone? I can't see without my glasses! Everyone look for my glasses, please—they must be somewhere!' And Johanna Dohnal sobbed, 'My watch is more important! I want my watch! Shut up about your stupid glasses!' And then the maths master's voice cut through the hubbub. He was standing at the teacher's desk looking very angry. 'What on earth is all this?' he thundered. 'You must all have gone crazy!' And he lent weight to this supposition by banging the teacher's desk with the big blackboard compasses three times, so hard that the little Advent wreath which had been put up yesterday quivered and shook alarmingly, along with its four candles.

'Hey, look at that!' muttered Brainbox, who was kneeling on the floor feeling behind the radiator for Johanna's watch. 'What do you know? He *can* come into a room even if there's nobody to hold the door open for him!'

'Get back to your places at once!' bellowed the maths master. 'Anyone not back at his desk in one second flat will do me twenty-four sums in his spare time!'

The maths master was the sort of person who commands respect. In circumstances that were even half-way normal, no one in 3D would have dared defy him. But present circumstances were not normal. Present circumstances were very far from normal indeed. Even Ferdi Dalmar, who held the door open and bowed and scraped and in the opinion of

44

3D was under the maths master's thumb, did not go back to his place. Ferdi Dalmar had just emptied the waste paper basket and was rummaging about among the orange peel and pencil shavings and crumpled paper for Johanna Dohnal's watch. The one concession 3D made to the presence of a person who commanded respect was to inform him, in chorus: 'Johanna Dohnal's lost her watch and we're helping her look for it!'

The maths master might not be a friendly teacher, but he was a clever one, the sort who knows exactly when shouting at a class will work and when it won't. And as the maths master liked to boast that no pupil had ever yet 'persisted in his disobedience' when spoken to sharply by himself, the maths master, and he did not want to lose his reputation for keeping discipline, he gave up shouting. Carefully adopting a softer, normal tone of voice, he moved away from the teacher's desk, approached the raised bottoms of 3D as it crawled around the floor looking for the watch, and asked for further information. He learned that Johanna Dohnal had come to school with a brand new gold watch that morning, and had taken it off during the previous lesson, which was Religious Studies, because its expanding gold chain bracelet was too tight for her fat wrist. 'It was cutting off my circulation,' sobbed Johanna, 'and my fingers were swelling up and getting pins and needles!' So she had put the watch down on her desk in the little hollow meant for pens and pencils. Martina, Thomas Huber, Ferdi Dalmar and Susi Kratochwil came over to admire the watch at break. 'But I know for certain it was still there afterwards,' sobbed Johanna.

'And when did you miss it?' asked the maths teacher.

'Well, then I took my orange peel over to the waste paper basket, and when I came back my watch was gone!' said Johanna Dohnal. Her voice was hoarse with sobbing, and she was so upset she had hiccups too, and her eyelids were swollen and pink with tears.

'And who was not at his desk when Johanna was on her way to and from the waste paper basket?' asked the maths master.

Not surprisingly, it turned out that none of 3D had been at their desks during ten o'clock break, and nobody knew exactly where he or she had been at the moment in question either.

'Oh, please, *please* can we go on looking, sir?' begged Johanna Dohnal. 'I can't go home without my watch, I can't!'

'Ladies and gentlemen,' said the maths master, folding his arms, 'ladies and gentlemen, I think we will go about this another way! As Johanna's watch was still here ten minutes ago, and nobody has left the room—or *did* anybody leave the room?' 3D stopped searching, looked at the maths master, and shook their heads. 'Very well,' the maths master went on. 'As nobody has left the room, then the watch must be here somewhere!'

'That's why we're looking,' said Brainbox, chucking Wolfgang Hahn his glasses, which he had just found behind the radiator.

The maths master dismissed this. 'As far as I'm aware, yours is the class in which all these thefts have been taking place! We can scarcely suppose that a gold watch has slipped down a crack in the floorboards, or found its way into the waste paper basket!' There was a murmur of agreement. 'Therefore,' the maths master went on, 'you will now all go back to your places and we will conduct an exhaustive search of your persons and your pockets!'

'What's exhaustive mean?' asked Ace, brushing dust off his trouser legs.

'Thorough, you ignorant Ass,' Thomas Huber told him,

and Ferdi Dalmar put up his hand and said they didn't have to exhaust the waste paper basket, he'd exhausted it already and there wasn't any gold watch inside.

'Back to your places, for a start,' said the maths master, and 3D obediently trooped back to their desks. 'Now, turn out all your pockets and put the contents on your desk tops!'

Brainbox got two half-price tram tickets and a piece of used chewing gum out of the breast pocket of his shirt, whispering to Lizzie, 'Is he actually *allowed* to search us, do you think?'

Lizzie shrugged her shoulders. 'Who cares?' she whispered back. 'Maybe he'll find the thief—and even if he doesn't it'll take up the maths lesson.'

'Everybody wearing trousers turn your trouser pockets inside out!' the maths master went on. Brainbox rose from his chair and tried to get at the pockets of his jeans, but the jeans were a year old, and during that year Brainbox had put on quite a lot of weight around the middle. It took him ten minutes to do the zip up when he was getting dressed. Brainbox's jeans fitted him as tightly as a whalebone corset. You couldn't have slipped so much as a sheet of paper in between him and those jeans. He could not even get his little finger into his pocket.

Lizzie watched Brainbox's futile attempts to turn his trouser pockets inside out. She giggled. She thought Brainbox wore such tight jeans out of vanity, to make himself look slimmer. The fact was that Brainbox wore jeans two sizes too small for him because his mother allegedly didn't have any money for new ones. ('Allegedly' means that there were reasons for doubting this. She had enough money for a new living room wall unit, anyway. And a new carpet too.)

'Give it up!' whispered Lizzie, pointing to Brainbox's fat stomach, over which the jeans stretched tightly. 'Anyone can see you couldn't even fit the little knob for winding a watch in there!'

'Silence! No more talking!' snapped the maths master, and since he was cross with Lizzie and Brainbox for whispering, and they sat in the row by the window anyway, he added, 'Very well, I'll begin here!' and went over to Brainbox.

Brainbox showed him the chewing gum and the tram tickets, indicated his problem with his trouser pockets, and offered to take his jeans down so as to get at them that way, but the maths master agreed with Lizzie. 'Don't bother,' he said, in some alarm. 'I don't see you hiding a lady's watch complete with metal bracelet in there!' Then he told Brainbox to turn round, and he inspected the two dark blue squares on the washed-out seat of Brainbox's trousers. This was where the two back pockets had once been, but Brainbox's mother had used them to patch torn places on the trouser legs. Then Brainbox had to take his satchel out of his desk and turn it out. It had nothing in it but a number of exercise books and two detective stories, which caused the maths master to raise a disapproving eyebrow. Finally the maths master looked inside Brainbox's desk. That was empty too. 'Thank you,' said the maths master, 'you can sit down.' And he went on to Lizzie.

Lizzie was wearing a red sweater and a red pleated skirt. She had no pockets in either the skirt or the sweater, as the maths master observed, nodding. Lizzie took her satchel out of her desk. It was full to bursting. She emptied it of several books and exercise books, a crochet hook and some pink wool, a stuffed toy dog the size of a rat, a hairbrush, a Donald Duck comic, several hair slides with plastic flowers on them, a tiny viewer for looking at slides, and seven beer mats.

'Please, that's all,' said Lizzie.

'Turn it upside down,' the maths master told her. Lizzie

48

hesitated. The maths master glared at her. 'Come along!' Lizzie picked up her satchel and turned it upside down. Three marbles clattered to the floor, a pingpong ball went bouncing through the classroom, there was a drift of pencil sharpenings followed by tiny bits of paper.

'Disgusting!' said the maths master. 'And a girl's satchel, too! I hope you are ashamed of yourself!' Then he bent down to look in Lizzie's desk, and flinched away from it in horror. 'Good God, what's *this*?' he exclaimed. 'Take it out at once, please!'

Bright red in the face, Lizzie took a number of mouldy old cheese sandwiches out of her desk. 'Now I know what the stink is over there,' muttered Ferdi Dalmar.

However, as there was nothing in Lizzie's desk but eight dried-up, curling, greasy, green-spotted cheese sandwiches and four brown apple cores, no gold watch, she was told she could sit down again. Martina Mader gave Lizzie a plastic bag, and she put the cheese sandwiches and apple cores in it. The maths master went on to Ace. It didn't take long to search Ace's desk, since he didn't hold with having a lot of unnecessary school stuff. He used an old green shoe-bag for a satchel, and it was empty. There was a ballpoint pen on his desk, and a maths exercise book and a notepad inside it. Ace himself, however, took a lot of searching. Ace was wearing a very splendid new boiler suit, with zips on the chest, hips, bottom and sleeves. There were even zips on the legs, both above and below the knees. Ace had fourteen zips in all on his boiler suit, not counting the zip doing up his flies, with which no one was concerned just now, and there was a pocket behind each of them. Ace obediently undid zip after zip, and turned out all the pockets, and the maths master inspected them. When Ace had removed the contents of the final pocket, one of the pockets on the knees, he had the following lying on his desk: two half-cigarettes and one

49

quarter-cigarette, nineteen Austrian schillings, a handful of paperclips, several rubber bands, half a pair of nail scissors, two throat pastilles without their wrappings, four little books of matches, five sheets of best lavatory paper and eight small boxes of pins. (They contained Ace's pin collection. He had been collecting pins for years. Sub-standard or unusual pins. Pins with heads that were too big, too small or otherwise misshapen, too broad or too long or drop-shaped. Pins where the pin itself was too long or too short, and pins of unusual colours. His most precious possession was a very long pin with an oval head that had pinky brown spots on it.)

The maths master viewed Ace's eight little boxes with some surprise. But he evidently liked collections, even peculiar ones. Remarking that he collected tin soldiers himself, he passed on. Ace put his possessions back in the pockets of his boiler suit and did the zips up.

Now it was His Nibs's turn. He took his blue blazer off, held it upside down and shook it. Nothing fell out except the folded white handkerchief from his breast pocket. Then His Nibs turned the side pockets of his smart trousers inside out. They hung from his hips like rabbit's ears. 'I'm afraid that's all the pockets I've got, sir,' he said. 'People aren't wearing trousers with back pockets just now. They're out of fashion.'

'Satchel, please,' sighed the maths master. The exhaustive search seemed to be getting him down.

His Nibs took his pale calfskin briefcase out of his desk. He held with unnecessary school stuff even less than Ace. There was nothing in the briefcase but half an eraser and a bar of chocolate with raspberry filling.

'Open your desk.' The maths master bent down, looked inside, and was about to straighten up again when he suddenly said, 'Wait a minute!' He put his hand inside the desk and brought out something checked brown and white and about the size of a cigarette packet. The brown and white thing was a handkerchief folded up like a parcel with a rubber band round it. The maths master felt the little parcel, and his eyes began to gleam.

'That's not mine,' said His Nibs, looking at the little parcel. 'I don't know whose it is. I've never seen it before.'

The maths master took the rubber band off the checked parcel and unfolded the handkerchief. It contained Johanna Dohnal's watch. You could have heard one of Ace's pins drop in the classroom. (The silence was broken twice by Johanna herself hiccuping, but nobody noticed that, what with all the tension.)

His Nibs stared at the shiny watch lying there in the check handkerchief. He looked horrified. His long eyelashes were fluttering, his hands were shaking, and his milky-coffee-coloured face had gone olive green.

'Well, Tabor? Have you any explanation of this?' asked the maths master.

His Nibs just stared at the watch and said nothing.

'Come along, speak up, Tabor!' said the maths master, but His Nibs didn't.

The rest of the class began muttering and whispering. Somebody told Johanna Dohnal, who was very short-sighted, that the maths master had just found her watch in His Nibs's desk.

'What, Nibs?' cried Johanna. 'Who'd have thought it! Fancy Nibs doing a thing like that! But it fits—he *did* come past my desk at break!'

'Silence! I want complete silence, please!' The maths master's voice did indeed silence both Johanna Dohnal and the mutterers and whisperers.

'Put your jacket on,' the maths master told His Nibs. 'You and I are going to see the Head. Michael Hanak, you can look after the class while I'm gone.'

His Nibs put his blazer on, bent down, picked up his folded white handkerchief and put it back in the breast pocket.

'And no delaying tactics, Tabor, if you please!' said the maths master. He took hold of His Nibs's arm. 'Come along, come along!'

For a split second it looked as if His Nibs were going to tear himself free and run away, but then he walked slowly out of the classroom with the maths master. He was holding his head in a very funny way, raised extremely high and looking at the ceiling.

If you hadn't noticed that his idea was to stop the tears rolling out of his eyes, it would have looked as if he were striding away, his head held proudly high, or something noble of that sort.

Chapter 6

which is a very short one, containing nothing but Brainbox's diary entry for the afternoon of December 1st. It was written in red ballpoint and handwriting even worse than Brainbox used on November 12th.

1st December

I've tried ringing His Nibs at home at least ten times, but there's nobody there. Of course, His Nibs could be at home and not answering the telephone, but I'm more inclined to think he's gone to his mother's wool shop and he's sitting around there feeling miserable.

Of course, he may not have told his mother anything about the whole wretched business. I wouldn't tell my mother anything if it had happened to me, not of my own free will. She'd only weep and wail and make a fuss, and she might well tell me to look her in the eye and say if I was sure it wasn't me. Over the years, I've noticed that my mother doesn't trust me much.

But His Nibs has quite a different sort of mother. His mother has eyes like Susi Kratochwil's Siamese cat, and she's really beautiful, and nearly always smiling. If I had a mother like that I'd go straight to her and tell her all about it and let her comfort me.

Yes, I'm sure His Nibs is at the wool shop. I could ring there, of course, but I don't know the number, and I can't find it in the telephone book. I've an idea it's in the phone book under Nibs's granny's name. She's his mother's mother, and I don't know what her surname is.

I don't think I behaved well at school today. When the maths master took His Nibs away I ought to have got up and said Nibs isn't a thief. I don't suppose it would have helped, but that's what I ought to have done. Only I was sort of paralysed by the shock.

I can't make that excuse for next break, though. I ought to have gone to the Head's office then. I don't know what I could have done then, either, but His Nibs is my friend. I should have stood up for him.

53

I was just too cowardly and timid! They'll only throw me out, I thought, they won't even let me get to see the Head! But you can't tell for sure, can you, if you haven't tried? They might have let me see the Head, they might not have thrown me out! And if they had thrown me out at least Nibs would have known I was on his side.

Ace and Lizzie didn't do anything for His Nibs either. We all just waited for him to come back into the classroom. And we were seething with rage at the way the others were going on. They all assumed straight off His Nibs must be the thief. Even Michi Hanak thought so, and I've always thought Michi Hanak was all right.

'Well, the watch was in his desk,' he told me. 'I don't see how you can get around that.'

And I heard horrible Susi Kratochwil tell Rosalind, 'I should think it's a gang—him and that silly Ace!' (Thank goodness Ace didn't hear her himself.) And Robert Sedlak had the nerve to say he'd suspected His Nibs all along, because His Nibs was so keen to cast suspicion on the boys in 3A, or someone in another class.

I could murder the lot of them! They're all against him, except for Lizzie and Ace. Oh, and Anna Trautenstein-Ebersthal, because she's never for or against anyone, she opts out entirely. Just sits there all pale and fair-haired and does enough work to get marked 'Satisfactory', and takes no notice of anything much. But I bet she wouldn't be for His Nibs either.

I can't make out why His Nibs didn't come back to the classroom. I mean, it was only just after ten when the maths master took him off, and when I finally went to the Head's office at twelve, in fourth break, to find out more, His Nibs had left. The secretary told me she didn't know anything about it, she hadn't come to work until eleven herself because of going to the dentist with her wisdom tooth, and at the moment, she said, there was a representative selling blinds in with the Head showing him patterns, because the Parents' Association is buying new blinds for the chemistry lab.

Can they simply have expelled him from school?

No. No, you can't expel a person just like that, and anyway the

Head wouldn't do it, he's not that sort.

I took His Nibs's briefcase home with me, and I felt so miserable I ate his bar of chocolate out of it.

Now I'm going to try ringing Nibs again, and if he still doesn't answer I'll ring Lizzie and Ace, and we'll all three go to the wool shop. I know where it is all right.

Not that I like chasing about the place. I'd rather sit and think. But I can't think properly when I don't know what's happening to His Nibs, and if you can't think then it's time to get up and do something!

Chapter 7

in which Lizzie stands up for children's rights, and Brainbox realizes how badly His Nibs needs a little help from his friends.

Brainbox dialled His Nibs's number at least a dozen times more, and each time he let the phone ring at least a dozen times before he hung up, and then he rang Ace and arranged to meet him at the tram stop at four o'clock. Then he got out his notebook and looked up Lizzie's number. He rang her so seldom that he didn't know it by heart.

Lizzie's mother answered the phone. She rambled on in a friendly way, thanking Brainbox for being so kind and helping Lizzie with her maths, and she said wouldn't he like to come and have coffee some time?

''Scuse me, please, Frau Schmelz,' said Brainbox, interrupting Lizzie's mother's gush, 'but can I speak to Lizzie? It's urgent.' So Lizzie's mother called her to the phone. 'Lizzie,' said Brainbox, 'we've got to *do* something about His Nibs. We'll meet at the tram stop at four, okay? Ace is coming too.'

Lizzie hesitated, but only for a moment, and then she said, 'Okay, Brainbox, I'll be there!' And she hung up.

Lizzie's mother was still hovering near the phone. 'You'll be where?' she asked.

'At the tram stop at four,' said Lizzie.

'And what's happening there?'

'We're going to do something about His Nibs,' Lizzie explained. 'Sort of prop him up, because he's feeling very low.'

'You'll do no such thing!' Lizzie's mother's voice was rising, in the shrill way Lizzie's father couldn't stand. 'Are you out of your mind? Mixing with a boy who's a thief?'

At lunch-time, Lizzie had told her mother exactly what had happened in the maths lesson, and her mother had listened, saying, 'Oh, how dreadful!' at frequent intervals. Lizzie had thought her mother thought it was dreadful for poor innocent Nibs to be under suspicion. Now she realized her mother hadn't understood any of it, and what she thought was dreadful was the fact that her daughter was friends with a boy who stole watches.

'But you know Nibs!' cried Lizzie. 'You know perfectly well he—'

'Oh no, I don't!' said her mother. 'One can never tell what a person's really like, and here's the living proof of it! You get a boy who seems nice and polite and well-man-nered, and he's really a thief the whole time!'

'He is *not* a thief!' cried Lizzie.

'Then how did the watch get into his desk?' asked her mother.

'Someone put it there!'

'Oh yes? And why did someone put it there?' Lizzie's mother shook her head. 'People steal things because they want them; they don't go putting them in among other people's possessions!'

Lizzie sighed impatiently. 'Look—the maths master said he was going to search the whole class. So the thief must have wanted to get rid of the watch in a hurry. So whoever it was—'

'Yes, and *who* was it?' her mother interrupted.

'*I* don't know, do I?' cried Lizzie.

'No, well, there you are!' Her mother shook her head again. 'It's too far-fetched, dear, this theory of yours.' And then she thought of something else. 'Do you remember when you lost your fountain pen at primary school, in the third year?' she asked. 'And when you took matchbox cars to

57

nursery school once or twice, and they disappeared too?'

'So what?' Lizzie didn't see what her mother was getting at. Her mother looked at her triumphantly. 'Why, this boy Nibs went to nursery school *and* primary school with you, didn't he?' she said.

This is the end, thought Lizzie. Calling him 'this boy Nibs' now, is she? Lizzie realized there was no hope of changing her mother's mind. She took off her indoor shoes and put on her red boots, which were standing beside the wardrobe.

'You're not really going to see him, are you?' asked her mother.

'Yes,' said Lizzie, putting on her warm jacket.

'Over my dead body!' said her mother. The hall of their apartment was a narrow one, and the big cupboards in it made it even narrower. Her mother was standing in between the cupboards, barring Lizzie's way to the front door. 'You are not going to see a boy who's a thief! And you most certainly are not going on a tram all by yourself! Do you want to end up like Günter?'

Günter was a man who lived in the apartment building next door. He had fallen off the step of a tram thirty years ago, and the second car of the tram, just behind it, had run over his legs.

'Look, I'm going to be thirteen in nine weeks' time,' said Lizzie, 'and there isn't a single thirteen-year-old in this whole city who isn't allowed to go on a tram on her own!'

'I don't care what the rest of them do!' screeched Lizzie's mother, and then, lowering her voice, she added, 'Darling, you know I worry about you. I never have a moment's peace when you're out alone, you *know* that!'

Lizzie knew that, all right. She had heard her mother say it day in, day out, and up till now it had made a difference to what she did.

Lizzie faced her mother, who was not very tall. Lizzie could look her in the face without having to tilt her own head back. There were tears in Lizzie's mother's eyes. This was a familiar sight to Lizzie too. And all of a sudden, as she stared her mother in the face, she saw imaginary pictures, like a reel of film running much too fast. Pictures of all the things she'd missed because of the tears in her mother's eyes: roller-skating with Ace, because her mother was afraid she'd break a leg. Open-air ice skating, because her mother thought the ice was too thin. Swimming in the river, because her mother thought the waterweeds were dangerous. No climbing trees, because her mother worried. No walks on her own, because her mother worried. No camping in the holidays, because her mother worried. No going to the cinema with Martina, because her mother worried . . . .

Lizzie switched off the reel of film racing through her mind and said, 'Let me by, Mum!'

Her mother put one hand on each of the cupboards by the walls of the hall so that she couldn't get past. 'I tell you what,' said her mother, 'we'll have tea now and then we'll go and buy you those nice blue boots, how about that?'

Lizzie shook her head. If it had just been a matter of her own amusement, she would probably have given in, as usual, and swapped her freedom for a pair of boots, so as not to feel guilty about worrying her mother. But it wasn't just herself, it was His Nibs. Nibs needed her. And she knew Brainbox and Ace wouldn't understand if she failed to turn up at the tram stop because of her mother's worries. 'Either you let me by,' said Lizzie firmly, 'or I'll call Dad and tell him you're being hysterical and kicking up a silly fuss again!'

It was much easier than Lizzie had expected. She didn't have to call her father at all. Her mother's arms dropped to her sides, leaving the way to the front door open to her. All she said was, 'When will you be back?'

Lizzie already had her hand on the door handle. 'I don't know,' she said, 'but not late. Whenever the others have to be home!'

Then she hurried out of the apartment and down the stairs. She felt as if she had grown a lot taller in the last ten minutes, at least a head taller than she had been that morning.

Ace and Brainbox were standing at the tram stop when Lizzie came running up at ten past four.

'Sorry,' gasped Lizzie. 'Took me a little longer than expected because—' But here she stopped. Somehow or other she felt it wouldn't be fair to her mother to tell them about the quarrel. It wouldn't be fair to His Nibs, either. His troubles were a lot more important just now.

'Well, you're here, that's the main thing,' said Ace, and then he told her he'd been to His Nibs's apartment and rung the doorbell so long and loud that he annoyed the woman next door. She had shot out of her own front door like a dog shooting out of its kennel, barking out the information that none of the Tabors was at home, they had all three gone out that morning and none of them was back yet, and if Ace went on ringing the bell all he'd do would be to drive their three cats crazy, cats have very sensitive hearing and can't stand that sort of noise without much mental suffering, she said.

'Perhaps Nibs is at his granny's,' said Lizzie. His Nibs was very fond of his granny, who was plump and round and rosy. Plump, round, rosy grandmothers are all very well in their way, thought Brainbox, but if I were Nibs and I had a cheerful, brown-skinned mother with eyes like a Siamese cat's that's where I'd take my troubles. 'I think we'd better try the wool shop first,' said Brainbox, and as Lizzie and Ace usually did what he said, they agreed.

Both Brainbox *and* Lizzie were right. His Nibs was in the
wool shop with his mother, and his granny was there too.
He was sitting in the back room of the shop looking
miserable. He hardly even said hullo to his friends. Lizzie,
Brainbox and Ace suddenly felt extremely useless and
superfluous. They didn't know what to say to him. They felt
it would be impertinent and nosy to ask what had happened
in the Head's office. Telling him they knew he was innocent
would be silly—he knew they knew! So the three of them just
stood around rather helplessly. His grandmother was in the
room behind the shop too. She pointed to her grandson. 'He
won't eat,' she said anxiously. 'Wouldn't have a thing for
lunch, nor tea either!' She picked a tray with some cake on it
up off a rack full of knitting wool. 'I got it specially for him,
too!' She looked sadly at the slices of cake. 'Here, children—
it's a shame to waste it,' she added. 'Help yourselves!'

Hesitantly, Lizzie and Brainbox and Ace helped themselves. They didn't actually want any cake, but it would give
Nibs's granny a little bit of pleasure if they ate it, and it
looked as if that was about the only thing they *could* do to
help just now.

When they had swallowed the cake somehow, and licked
their sticky fingers and wiped them on a tissue provided by
Nibs's granny Nibs himself finally raised his head and
asked, 'What do the others say about it?'

Lizzie and Ace looked at Brainbox. Brainbox took his
time over answering. What he said mattered. Mattered to
His Nibs enormously. Brainbox knew what His Nibs was
hoping to hear. He was wondering whether there was any
point in lying, but Lizzie broke in on his deliberations,
saying, 'Who cares *what* the others say?'

'They're just shits!' cried Ace.

'Good gracious, children, what language!' said Nibs's granny, horrified.

'Sorry,' muttered Ace, 'but it's true!'

'You idiot,' whispered Brainbox. 'Why did you have to go telling him?'

'It's only what I thought, anyway,' said His Nibs, and he went on staring mournfully into space.

The little cowbell on the shop door rang. The lady who had been buying a big pack of rug-making wool, thus keeping His Nibs's mother in the front of the shop, was just leaving.

His Nibs's mother came and stood in the open doorway of the room behind the shop. 'It's very sweet of you to come,' she told the children. 'He thinks everyone in his class must think he's the thief.'

'Well, they do,' said His Nibs.

'We don't!' Lizzie protested.

'The others do, though,' His Nibs muttered, kicking a stack of knitting wool boxes. The stack swayed. His Nibs's mother darted forward and caught it, meanwhile casting Brainbox an inquiring glance. The glance was inquiring: is he right?

Brainbox nodded. 'Please, you must go up to school, Frau Tabor!' he told her. 'Go and tell the Head—'

'I've already been up to school,' said His Nibs's mother, interrupting. 'They rang me straight away, at ten o'clock, and I went up to school directly.'

'What happened?' asked Lizzie.

The cowbell on the shop door rang again. 'A customer,' murmured His Nibs's mother, but the person who had come into the shop was not a customer, it was His Nibs's father. And he was whistling the march from *The Bridge on the River Kwai* as he vaulted over the counter so as to take a short cut to the room behind the shop.

The doorway to the room behind the shop was low, and His Nibs's father, who was extremely tall, had to bend to go through it. 'Good heavens, the place is full of people!' he said. 'So full I can't spot my own young thief. Where is he, then?'

'I'm here,' said His Nibs, trying to smile and failing. The smile just twitched across his face like a nervous tic. His father made his way past his mother, Lizzie, His Nibs's granny, Ace, Brainbox and the cardboard cartons full of knitting wool until he reached Nibs himself. 'Hi there, my old pickpocket,' he said, running his hand through his son's black curls.

'Please!' said His Nibs's mother. 'This is much too serious for silly jokes!'

'It's much too serious for anything *but* silly jokes,' said His Nibs's father.

'Well, your sunny cheeriness isn't much use to him,' said His Nibs's mother, and His Nibs's father said, 'I'm stifling in this woolly mousehole—you can't breathe in here! Let's shut the shop and get out of this room. We can't talk properly if there's a customer coming in to be served every few minutes.'

'Quite true,' said Granny. She went out into the shop, hung a notice saying CLOSED in the door, locked it and pulled down the shutters over the door and the two shop windows. His Nibs's granny sat on the only chair in the shop, his mother perched on the counter, and his father, Nibs himself, Ace, Brainbox and Lizzie sat down on the soft carpet on the floor.

'Now, if I understand all this correctly,' said His Nibs's father, 'there's been a whole series of thefts in your class, and one of the teachers found Johanna Dohnal's gold watch on my son this morning, is that right?'

'It was actually in his desk,' said Lizzie. 'But anybody

63

could have put it there, what with all the confusion in the classroom just before.'

'And then what happened?' asked His Nibs's father, and everyone looked at His Nibs.

'The maths master took me to the Head,' said His Nibs, 'and the first thing the Head did was send someone to fetch Dr Hufnagel, because she's our form mistress. But Dr Hufnagel wasn't at school today, it was her day off. So then the Head asked me why I kept stealing things. And I said it wasn't me. And he said I only made it worse by lying.'

'Then what?' asked his father.

His Nibs shrugged his shoulders helplessly. 'I'm not sure now. They said they'd tell my parents and I ought to think it over and decide whether it wouldn't be better to admit the truth—and so on. And I didn't say anything else at all.' His Nibs was pulling strands of wool out of the shaggy carpet. 'Because I couldn't keep on and on and on saying I'd no idea how the watch got into my desk.'

'And then what?' It was his granny asking, this time.

'Then Mum came,' said His Nibs, and everyone looked at his mother and waited for her to go on. But she only murmured, 'I think I handled it badly.'

'How do you mean?' asked Granny.

'Mother, I told you at lunch-time!' said His Nibs's mother, rather crossly. She turned to her husband. 'And I told *you* over the telephone. I don't want to keep repeating it!'

'You were in such a state on the telephone I could hardly make a word out,' said His Nibs's father. 'Come on, tell us again, calmly. The children would like to hear about it too.'

'She's always so impulsive!' murmured Granny. 'Not tactful enough!'

His Nibs's mother drew her legs up on the counter, wrapped her arms round them and rested her chin on her knees. Her Siamese cat's eyes sparkled bright blue. 'It was only because I can't stand schools,' she said. 'And they always remind me of my own schooldays. How would any of you understand?' His Nibs's mother ran both hands through her close curls. 'A little black girl, an American soldier's daughter! I was the lowest of the low at school, that's what I was!' She took a deep breath. 'And when I got up to school today, *he* was sitting there'—here she pointed to His Nibs— 'and the Head and that maths master were going on as if *he* were the lowest of the low! And then it all sort of surged up in me, and I lost my temper. I lost it worse than I've ever lost it before. And I told them they were a bunch of Fascists and racists and idiots and—'

'Oh, dear heaven!' groaned His Nibs's father.

His mother went on. 'And then I took my son's hand and went off with him. Because I know what it's like when you're a child and you can't defend yourself.'

'And as we went out she told them they were senile old fogies!' said His Nibs. He seemed to be feeling a bit better, and managed a faint smile.

'Did you really?' asked his granny, running a knitting needle through her piled-up hair. 'My goodness, if you really said that you'll have to apologize!'

'Never mind that for the moment,' said His Nibs's father. 'Listen to this, which is much more important. I rang our solicitor, and he spoke to someone in the police, and the man in the police said that whole business of the search wasn't worth a brass farthing by way of proof. It wouldn't stand up in law anyway, for one thing, and for another thing too much time had elapsed between the theft and the search. And my son and his desk are not the same thing at all! It would be different if he'd had the watch in his socks or his underpants. But the fact is, they have absolutely no evidence against him and there's nothing they can do about it.' His

Nib's father seemed to feel that this cleared everything up, for he asked, 'Right—shall I open the shop again?'

His Nibs's mother shook her head. 'Proof or no proof, they still think he stole it,' she said.

'I'm not going back to school any more,' said His Nibs quietly.

His father took him by the shoulder and shook him very gently. 'Don't be ridiculous!' he said. 'What does it matter? *Let* the senile old fogies think you're a kleptomaniac if they like—you tell them to go take a running jump!'

'I'm sure Dr Hufnagel won't think you stole the watch,' said Lizzie.

'Or Herr Huber who teaches gym either,' said Ace. 'He likes you.'

'And they *can't* accuse you of doing unsatisfactory work,' said Brainbox, 'not with the sort of marks you get!'

'But all the rest of the class think I did it!' shouted His Nibs, pulling frantically at strands of carpet. 'That's what I can't bear!'

'Would you like to go to another school instead?' asked his father.

'No, I wouldn't!' shouted His Nibs, and he tugged so hard that bits of carpet went flying through the air.

'Listen, there's no other alternative,' said his father. He looked round, expecting everyone to back him up. No one said anything. His Nibs began to sob. Brainbox closed his eyes, put his thumb in his mouth and thought. Having principles is fine, he thought, and one of my absolutely basic principles was that I didn't care two hoots about all this silly stealing business. But you need to be able to abandon your principles to help a friend. 'I'll find out who really stole the watch,' said Brainbox, 'and then it'll all be cleared up.'

'Do you think you can?' His Nibs's mother was looking doubtfully at Brainbox with her bright blue eyes.

66

'I can't say I'll actually *enjoy* it,' Brainbox told her, 'but yes, I do think I can solve the problem.'

Chapter 8

in which we print more extracts from Brainbox's diary, and he narrows down the list of suspects quite considerably by a process of logical thought.

1st December (11 p.m.)

My mother has just knocked on my door for the fourth time to say isn't it about time I went to sleep, but seeing I've just thrown one of my basic principles overboard I'd better get something written down in the way of the principles I'm keeping, before I set about the nasty, mean, beady-eyed business of playing detective.

1. I like His Nibs. I'd like him even if he was really the thief.

2. I've got nothing against the real thief either. I don't know why he steals things. I'm not making any judgments before I know more about it.

3. I don't think stealing is a good thing or a clever thing, but I know worse things do happen.

If somebody punches me in the face when I've done nothing to hurt him it's worse than if somebody steals something from me (and I can tell, because both of those have happened to me). I'm fonder of myself than my property.

4. The only reason I'm trying to find the thief is to help His Nibs. If he wasn't a friend of mine I'd get on with reading the new Asterix book, and I couldn't care less about thieves and thefts and who really dunnit!

2nd December

His Nibs wasn't at school today. His mother told me on the telephone he's refusing to go. And he doesn't want to see anyone either. Not even us. His mother said maybe he'll be feeling psychologically stronger tomorrow.

68

His father has been to see the Head. I saw him at ten o'clock break, and there was an elderly gentleman with him. That was the Tabors' solicitor, so His Nibs's mother told me on the phone. He'd come to tell the Head where he got off—well, that's how she put it. But she didn't know exactly what her husband and the solicitor and the Head had said to each other. She said her husband didn't ring her till mid-day, and then he did nothing but crack silly jokes. However, he's just putting that on, I'm sure he is. To make His Nibs and His Nibs's mother feel better. Because when he marched into the Head's office at school he didn't look as if he thought it was a bit funny. His face was set and furious!

The atmosphere in 3D is much the same as before. They even say the fact that His Nibs didn't come to school proves he's guilty. I hoped and hoped, all morning, something else would be stolen. That would be the simplest way of proving him innocent. But unfortunately nobody lost a thing today.

Lizzie's trying the soft approach. She thinks she can convince most of the girls His Nibs is innocent, because the girls have always been so keen on him. She had a go at Babsi Binder and Katherina Rösch in break today. She talked and talked to them, and she thinks success is in sight. Well, I wish her luck, but I don't agree with her—I know those silly cows! Ace is taking a tough line. He's going around saying he'll thump anyone who says a word against His Nibs. But that just makes the others feel surer they're right. Specially knowing Ace really is strong enough to flatten the lot of them.

So now I'm getting down to work. In a quiet, secret sort of way, which I don't like a bit. And in a hurry too, which I like even less. But we haven't got much time to play with, seeing His Nibs refuses to come back to school before it's all cleared up. I'm afraid the Head might expel him for deliberately staying away from work. . .I believe he could *do that.*

There are probably a number of different ways of approaching and solving this case, but as I'm the sort who'd rather sit down than chase around, always supposing I can't actually lie *down, I'm going to start*

69

by doing as much of the job as I can on paper.

Right: Lizzie and Ace and I start by assuming that all the things were stolen by the same person. That doesn't have to be so, but it seems probable. In fact, just thinking of the ghastly possibility of six different thieves gives me the horrors. We'd never get anywhere! No, I'm looking for a single thief, and by now we can be sure it's someone in our class.

So the full list of suspects runs like this—actually it's the class register. I copied it down.

Ammerling, Daniel (Brainbox)
Berger, Ferdi
Binder, Babsi
Böck, Heinzi
Dalmar, Ferdi
Dohnal, Johanna
Elterlein, Otto (Ace)
Fröhlich, Rosalind
Habersack, Regine
Hahn, Wolfgang
Hanak, Michael
Huber, Thomas
Kirchner, Doris
Knoblich, Andrea
Knopf, Andreas
Kratochwil, Susi
Lehmann, Klaus
Mader, Martina
Moser, Trixi
Prihoda, Ivan
Rösch, Katherina
Schmelz, Lizzie
Schmied, Oliver
Schmitt, Achim

Schneider, Egon
Schütz, Daniela
Sedlak, Robert
Tabor, Michael (His Nibs)
Trautenstein-Ebersthal, Anna
Wehrle, Otto

Okay, that's the whole long list of everyone in 3D, so now to weed them out. For a start, the 'flu epidemic in 3D was at its worst the day Lizzie's purse was stolen. I looked in the register at school today, and the people absent that day were:

Binder, Böck, Fröhlich, Hanak, Knoblich, Knopf, Moser, Schneider, Schütz and Wehrle.

So those ten people away with 'flu can't have stolen the purse. That seems to be perfectly clear!

Lizzie just looked in. She strikes me as a bit pale. I think she's having quite a bit of trouble with her mother, because of insisting on getting more freedom. But I don't think she wants to talk about it, so I don't ask questions.

Lizzie says I ought to cross her off my list of suspects as well as the ten people who were away with 'flu, because I can't seriously think she stole her own money and then kicked up a fuss about it.

She has a point there.

So that takes eleven names off my list, leaving me with exactly nineteen.

And now I come to look at them, I can cross three more names out. The day the milk money and Rosalind's fifty schillings disappeared Anna Trautenstein-Ebersthal and Doris Kirchner were absent, according to the register. And so neither of them can have been the thief. Nor can Martina Mader—she won't have pinched the milk money herself, will she?

Right, now for the next bit.

The day Ivan Prihoda lost his golden chain the only people in the class absent were Anna Trautenstein-Ebersthal and Klaus

Lehmann—again, according to the register. But the fact that it was stolen from the boys' changing-room next to the gym means that the thief has to be a boy. Girls aren't allowed in our changing-room, any more than barmaids are allowed into monasteries.

So we can also remove the names of Klaus Lehmann and all the girls in the class from the list of suspects. And Ivan Prihoda's name too, since he wouldn't have stolen his own chain unless he was cracked, which he isn't, and anyway I was next to those jeans of his all through break, keeping an eye on them without knowing it. So the theft has to have taken place during the gym lesson, and Ivan had been told off for misbehaviour and spent the entire lesson standing in one corner of the gym, and he never moved from the spot.

Lizzie thinks I must be able to remember who went out to the changing-room during gym that day, but I can't. Because I hate doing gym, so I just think of something else and let it all wash over me in a kind of haze.

Ace has just come in to join me and Lizzie. He's sitting right beside me, and he can't remember exactly who left the gym that day either, because there was so much coming and going. A ball hit Oliver Schmied on the nose, and he had a nosebleed, and one or two people went to get handkerchiefs, and then Herr Huber said the handkerchiefs ought to be wet to stop the bleeding, and some more people went out to put them under the tap. Ace thinks he has vague memories of who went to fetch handkerchiefs and put them under the tap, but we're not going in for vague memories. We're going to stick to hard facts, and this seems a good point to list the people left as suspects, i.e. not counting Klaus Lehmann (absent), Ivan Prihoda (theft victim) or any of the girls.

The list now runs: Daniel Ammerling (Brainbox), Ferdi Berger, Ferdi Dalmar, Otto Elterlein (Ace), Wolfi Hahn, Thomas Huber, Oliver Schmied, Achim Schmitt, Robert Sedlak and Michael Tabor (His Nibs).

So now we're down to ten!

Ace says he's going to thump me for leaving him on the list of suspects, and Lizzie says there's no sense in leaving Nibs on the list when we're trying to prove he wasn't the thief. Okay, okay! But then I might as well cross myself out too, seeing I'm one hundred per cent certain I'm not the thief. And we can cross out Achim Schmitt too. He wasn't at school on the day of the last theft, when Johanna lost her gold watch. He had the day off to go to his father's wedding. (His father wasn't marrying his mother this time, he was marrying somebody else.)

So the remaining suspects are: Ferdi Berger, Ferdi Dalmar, Wolfi Hahn, Thomas Huber, Oliver Schmied and Robert Sedlak.

Now let's go back to Susi's birthday party and compare the list of suspects with the list of people from our class at the party when the savings book was stolen.

Possible thieves: Berger, Dalmar, Hahn, Huber, Schmied, Sedlak.

Party guest (boys only): Böck, Dalmar, Hahn, Hanak, Huber, Knopf, Schneider, Sedlak.

Ferdi Berger wasn't at the party, so he isn't the thief.

Ferdi Dalmar is still a suspect.

So is Wolfi Hahn.

So is Thomas Huber.

Oliver Schmied wasn't at the party.

But Robert Sedlak was.

Which leaves us with four prime suspects: Ferdi Dalmar, Wolfgang Hahn, Thomas Huber and Robert Sedlak.

And here the three of us sit, goggling at this list. 'Amazing!' mutters Lizzie, for about the twelfth time. As for Ace, he wants it to be Thomas Huber, of course, because he can't stand Thomas Huber!

Lizzie and Ace have just gone. Lizzie had to go because she wants to get her mother used to her new-found independence gradually. (Her father asked her to do it gradually, to keep his wife from having a nervous breakdown.) Ace had to go and fetch his sister from nursery school. Well, he doesn't actually have to fetch her—he really wants to. He has this very soft spot for his little sister.

And I'm still sitting here staring at those four names, and I catch myself out hoping one of them in particular is the thief. And just now I told Ace he mustn't suspect Thomas Huber more than the rest, which is perfectly understandable because Thomas is his enemy and keeps calling him Ass. But the only reason I want Ferdi Dalmar to be the thief is because I'd think it was funny for such a wet, feeble sort of teacher's pet to go in for something like stealing!

Yuk! I knew it all along! Once you start playing the boy detective and thinking sneaky thoughts and sniffing about for clues and setting traps, you've lost half your ordinary nice friendliness. And seeing you haven't got all that much of it to start with, the half that's left doesn't go quite far enough.

Oh, I'm going to watch TV. I've had about enough of this for one day, and it's given me a headache. I hope it's not a thriller on television. I hope it's a nice soppy love story, without any crime or violence except maybe a suicide when we get to the happy ending!

Chapter 9

in which Ace and Lizzie start something Brainbox doesn't like at all, and Dr Hufnagel expresses an opinion about thieves which he does like a lot.

December 3rd was a horrible day at school, being a Friday, and on Fridays 3D's timetable went as follows: maths, Latin, English, German, biology. Not a period among them when you could have a nice rest, relax the brain, daydream, play Battleships or make paper aeroplanes.

His Nibs didn't come to school that day, either, and nobody talked about anything except the gold watch at break, or about anybody except His Nibs. Except when Ace marched up to a gossiping group, looking very threatening. Then discussion of His Nibs and the watch would die down, only to start up again once he went off.

In the first period, maths, the maths master didn't mention the absence of His Nibs or the search of 3D the day before yesterday. All he said was, 'Considering the time we wasted in your last lesson, we'll have to work at twice the usual speed today!' Then he picked up the chalk and went to the board and did sums on it, so fast that even the people in the class who were good at maths couldn't keep up. So the majority of 3D stopped trying after ten frantic minutes, gave up copying off the board, and passed their time quietly as best they might, drawing little matchstick men, counting off the seconds, decorating their maths books, pushing back their cuticles or soaking up ink with blotting paper. But none of this was relaxing. It was their way of reacting to what is called a stress situation. After all, the maths master might turn round any minute and catch someone engaged in these unmathematical activities, and then there'd be hell to pay.

The second lesson was Latin, and the third was English, with a young lady from Liverpool trying to talk to 3D very slowly, so that everyone could appreciate her beautiful English way of saying 'th' and do their best to copy it. The young lady from Liverpool thought the best way to learn a foreign language was by total immersion in it, so she went on and on in English, not a word of German, entirely ignoring the limited extent of 3D's English vocabulary. The result was that at the end of the lesson, Ace thought he had been listening to the sad story of an auctioned horse, while Lizzie said no, it was a story of a haunted house, and Thomas Huber was ready to swear it was the story of a horse in a house, and the lady from Liverpool had just been telling them an English version of a chapter from *Pippi Longstocking*.

After these guessing games, it was break. Lizzie stayed at her desk, writing something on a pink postcard in small letters.

'Hullo, Lizzie—given up trying to win the girls over, have you?' asked Brainbox. Lizzie nodded. 'No point in it,' she said sadly. 'You were right again! While I'm actually going on at them, they act as if they believed me, but somebody else only has to come along and say the opposite and then they believe him instead!' Lizzie sighed, and concentrated on the little pink postcard again.

Brainbox looked at her in surprise. 'What on earth is that, Lizzie love?' he asked.

Lizzie handed him the postcard, with a grin. Ace leaned over from the desk behind, with an even broader grin. The writing on the pink postcard said: MEET ME AT 3.10 THIS AFTERNOON OUTSIDE MÜLLER'S BRIDAL WEAR!

'Who do you want to meet you outside Müller's Bridal

Wear at 3.10 this afternoon?' asked Brainbox.

'Thomas Huber!' said Lizzie, giggling, and then she explained. She was planning to be very, very good friends with Thomas Huber from now on. She could work it easily, because Thomas had been in love with her for ages, anyway, and he passed her a note at least once a week begging her to meet him somewhere after school in secret. Well, now she was finally going to be kind and do as he asked.

'But you don't like Thomas Huber!' said Brainbox. 'You've always laughed at his love letters!'

Lizzie nodded. 'That's right,' she said. 'Still, it can't be helped.'

And she explained that she was planning to be so friendly with Thomas Huber because Ace thought Thomas was the thief. 'If I make friends with him I can watch him and ask him questions,' said Lizzie. 'And Ace says if I'm clever enough about it Thomas Huber will give himself away!'

'Oh, Lizzie!' groaned Brainbox. He was so horrified he had gooseflesh on his arms. 'Oh no! That really is the end!'

'You think so?' Lizzie looked unhappy. She was on the point of tearing up the little pink postcard when Ace shoved his oar in. 'What *I* call the end is someone smuggling a gold watch into His Nibs's desk!' he said. 'It's all very well being frank and straightforward, Brainbox, but if you're investigating something grubby like this you can't always keep your own hands clean, can you?'

'Was this your idea, Ace?' asked Brainbox.

'Sure!' said Ace, grinning. 'I'm not ashamed of it either! Have *you* got a better notion?'

Brainbox said nothing.

'Well, there you are, then!' said Ace, triumphantly. 'We've got to do *something*, right?' And he nodded to Lizzie. Lizzie folded the pink card until it was no bigger than a postage stamp, and then she picked up a pencil and a pencil

77

sharpener and strolled over to the waste paper basket, swaying her hips. As she passed Thomas Huber's desk, she dropped the folded card on it.

Brainbox was watching Thomas Huber. He watched him unfold the card, he watched him read it, and he saw the ecstatic smile that lit up Thomas's face all of a sudden. He also saw Thomas turn round and look happily in the direction of the waste paper basket, where Lizzie was standing sharpening her pencil, the picture of innocence.

'It's not fair,' Brainbox told Ace, in an undertone.

Ace ran both hands through his bristly red hair and frowned. There were deep frown lines on his freckled forehead. 'He wasn't fair to Nibs, either,' he said.

'Oh, do stop it!' snapped Brainbox. 'He's only one of our four suspects!'

'Until we've proved otherwise,' muttered Ace, turning away.

Brainbox felt his temper rising. He was really beginning to boil! And as this very seldom happened to him, and he wasn't used to the sensation, he did not like it a bit. It was like getting sudden bad toothache or appendicitis. Brainbox felt quite unable to answer Ace. He didn't feel able to speak to Lizzie, either, when she came back from sharpening her pencil, sat down, and said, with satisfaction, 'He took the bait! Just look at him beaming!'

Brainbox waited for his horrible feeling of anger to die down. He waited in silence, with his eyes shut and his thumb in his mouth. By the time Dr Hufnagel came into the classroom his anger had died down quite a lot. It felt no worse than an itch in the navel or a sore gum.

First of all Dr Hufnagel wrote something in the register. Everyone was waiting in suspense to hear what she was going to say, because obviously, as 3D's form mistress, she had to say *something* about the affair of the watch. After she

78

had marked His Nibs absent in the register, she closed it, went over to the window, and looked at the sleet outside. 'Wants to gain time,' whispered Lizzie. She timed Dr Hufnagel by the second hand of her watch. Dr Hufnagel stood by the window for a full minute before she turned round and said that as their form mistress she had something to discuss with 3D. Then she went to His Nibs's desk, sat on it, and said she wanted to make it quite clear, once and for all, that no one, absolutely no one, was entitled to call Michael Tabor a thief. There was nothing like enough evidence!

After a split second of surprised silence, the class began to murmur, their murmurs eventually rising to loud protest.

'But my watch was in his desk!' cried Johanna Dohnal.

'Who else could it have been?' asked Oliver Schmied.

''Course it was him! I said so from the start!' shouted Robert Sedlak.

But Dr Hufnagel shouted even louder. 'Be quiet! Be quiet at once!' she shouted. Then she added, 'It could have been anyone. Someone else may have put the watch in his desk.'

'Hear, hear!' said Ace, clapping loudly. Lizzie clapped too. Brainbox, who was still busy dealing with the remains of his anger, clapped less vigorously, but all the same they made enough noise to drown out the other children's protests.

Dr Hufnagel waited patiently until Ace and Lizzie got tired of clapping, and they and Brainbox stopped. Then she said one should never condemn anyone without absolutely clear proof of guilt. And Michael Tabor had always been nice to them, and it would be a good idea to try putting themselves in his place before they called him a thief.

'*I'm* not putting myself in a thief's place!' said Robert Sedlak, firmly.

'Nor am I!' said Babsi Binder, even more firmly.

Dr Hufnagel got off the desk. 'Very well, as you're not open to reason, we'll put an end to this conversation,' she said, and she went to the teacher's desk. 'Get your grammar books out and turn to page ninety-eight, please.' Then she looked at the two front desks by the window, where Brainbox, Ace and Lizzie were sitting, and said, 'If you see Michael Tabor, as I hope you will, then please will you tell him *I* don't think he's a thief?'

Brainbox, Ace and Lizzie nodded hard. 'Dr Hufnagel's all right!' Lizzie whispered. 'I feel better already!'

And Brainbox found himself able to speak to Lizzie again, and whispered back, 'Yes, Dr Hufnagel's great!'

After the German lesson, during which they analysed various kinds of subsidiary clause and the atmosphere between Dr Hufnagel and the majority of 3D was a distinctly frosty one, she left the room and leaned against the wall between the two corridor windows, opposite the classroom door. She was on corridor duty.

Break after the fourth period was only five minutes. Brainbox spent three of them with his eyes closed and his thumb in his mouth, coming to a decision. When he had reached his decision he got up and walked out of the room. Ace and Lizzie thought he needed to go to the lavatory, but he only crossed the corridor and leaned against the wall next to Dr Hufnagel.

She didn't notice him at all at first, because she was looking at a newspaper, and there was quite a lot of noise and running about in the corridor. Brainbox cleared his throat. When Dr Hufnagel still didn't notice him, he went a bit closer and coughed discreetly. This attracted her attention.

'Oh, hullo, Daniel,' she said. 'Nice of you to come and keep me company! Corridor duty is a dead bore!' She smiled, and indicated the thumb Brainbox was sucking.

80

'You know, sometimes I'm afraid you might consume that thumb of yours entirely, like an ice lolly.'

Brainbox took his thumb out of his mouth, inspected it carefully, and murmured, 'Don't worry, it'll last a good while yet.' Then, not much louder, he added, 'Dr Hufnagel, do you think it would be right to find out who the real thief was?'

'Good gracious, Daniel, do you know?' Dr Hufnagel's eyes were wide with curiosity.

'Not yet,' said Brainbox, 'but I think I soon will.'

Dr Hufnagel was getting quite excited. 'Did you see or hear anything? Have you got any kind of evidence—clues or so on?'

'No, only my thoughts,' said Brainbox, and she looked disappointed.

'I've always been able to rely on *them,* though,' said Brainbox. 'That's not my problem. My problem'—and here Brainbox put his thumb back in his mouth—'my problem is I'll probably feel sorry for the thief. He's a poor sort of person, so far as I can see. And not very happy.'

'But a thief, all the same,' said Dr Hufnagel.

'So what?' Brainbox looked hard at Dr Hufnagel. 'So what?' he repeated.

'Why, Daniel!' Dr Hufnagel was genuinely horrified. 'People can't just go about stealing things! How can you say a thing like that? And nobody in your class is so poor he *needs* to steal. I know quite a bit about all your home backgrounds.'

'That's not what I meant about being poor,' said Brainbox.

'What did you mean, then?'

Brainbox shrugged his shoulders. 'Don't really know just yet. It's only a kind of feeling.'

'None the less, Daniel,' said Dr Hufnagel, shaking her

head, 'one can't have someone in the class stealing. I mean, look at the state of affairs in your class at this moment! It can't go on!'

'No, sure,' agreed Brainbox. 'But I got this thought. I thought maybe a thief who steals for some peculiar reason of his own isn't really any worse than someone who runs another person in the class down for no reason, without any real proof. Or is that idea all wrong? And another thing I'd like to know is what will happen to the thief? What can *he* expect?'

The bell went for the end of break. The children in the corridor dispersed, and still Dr Hufnagel had not answered Brainbox's questions. Finally—and not until the biology master was in sight on the stairs—she said, 'I'm sorry, Daniel, but those are two very difficult things to answer. I'll have to think about them.'

Brainbox could well understand a person having to think. He nodded at Dr Hufnagel, and went back into the class-room with the biology master.

Chapter 10

in which Lizzie gets nowhere much with her detective work, and Lizzie's mother has the best idea for getting somewhere another time, though nobody but Brainbox notices.

Lizzie left the apartment just before three, smiling dreamily, and ran down the stairs. The dreamy smile was because it looked very much as if Lizzie's mother was gradually getting used to her going out on her own. When Lizzie left, she had been sitting in the living room perfectly dry-eyed, knitting a sweater with a Norwegian pattern in red and white wool. And though she did ask when Lizzie would be back, even Lizzie's father couldn't have said the voice in which she put that question reminded him of a screeching saw.

Down in the hall, Lizzie stopped by the door of the caretaker's apartment and took a tiny mirror and a lipstick out of her cape pocket. She painted her lips red, to make herself seem even more desirable to Thomas Huber. Inspecting the results of this cosmetic venture in the little mirror, she muttered crossly to herself, found a tissue and wiped the lipstick off again. Then she made her way to Müller's Bridal Wear.

Thomas Huber was already there. He smiled happily when he saw Lizzie coming. Then she came closer, and he asked, in some concern, 'Have you got a cold, Lizzie?' For Lizzie's upper lip and the tip of her nose were deep pink, owing to the fact that Lizzie had no more practice in removing lipstick than she had in applying it.

Oh no, said Lizzie, she hadn't got a cold, definitely not, and suddenly she felt rather silly. This, after all, was her very first date. Not so long ago her grandmother had remarked,

to her mother, 'Ah, you never forget your first date, do you?'
And Lizzie's mother had replied, 'My goodness, no! You're
so full of feelings at that age—it's as if the heavens were
opening before you!'

Glancing up Lizzie saw that the heavens were indeed
about to open, but only in order to shed either rain or snow
any moment. However, she was full of feelings all right.
They were a mixture of dislike of Thomas, uncertainty as to
how she was going to question him, and total helplessness
when she wondered how to make out she liked him all the
time. They added up to a feeling which was very deeply
unpleasant indeed. She also felt slightly annoyed because
Thomas had expressed his suspicion that she had a cold.
Lizzie did not think it was very polite to comment on a
young lady's pink upper lip and nose.

'Looks like rain,' said Thomas.

Lizzie nodded, trying to smile.

'Would you like to go to the cinema, Lizzie? They're
showing the Asterix film at the Metropolitan at four
o'clock.'

Going to the cinema won't get me anywhere, thought
Lizzie. You have to keep quiet in the cinema. I won't get any
confession out of Thomas there.

'I've already seen the Asterix film three times,' said
Lizzie, although she had not seen it at all, and would very
much have liked to.

'Then let's go into the city centre,' suggested Thomas.
'There are lots of cinemas there.' And he took a sheet of
newspaper out of his coat pocket. It listed the films being
shown that Friday, and he had marked those cinemas that
had matinée performances in red felt-tip pen.

'I haven't got any money for the cinema, anyway,' said
Lizzie.

'Oh, that's all right! I'll take you!' said Thomas.

'But the cinemas in the city centre are very expensive,' said Lizzie.

'Doesn't matter!' said Thomas Huber, beaming. 'I'm in funds!'

This was news indeed! Thomas Huber never had much money in the usual way; in fact, he was forever complaining that his parents were rolling in it, but they kept him so short he couldn't even buy a Disney comic, he could scarcely afford his daily chewing gum. So now, all of a sudden, he had enough money for two expensive cinema tickets? Three times his pocket money wouldn't cover that! But supposing he had pinched Rosalind's fifty schillings, and sold Ivan's chain and pendant, *then* he'd have money for two cinema tickets all right! Or was he planning to take her out with her own money? Maybe he was actually carrying her lost purse around with him!

Lizzie's eyes narrowed, and her nostrils quivered slightly. She felt like a hound picking up a scent—but then Thomas said, 'I had this amazing piece of luck, see? I was just going out when my uncle came in and asked where I was off to, and when I told him he gave me a hundred to take you out with!' Beaming all over his face, Thomas Huber reached under his coat and took a hundred-schilling note out of his trouser pocket. 'And I'd already made sure I'd got some money, anyway!' Reaching into his other trouser pocket, Thomas produced a spotted handkerchief tied up in a tiny bundle. 'I gutted my piggy bank—look, six tens!' And Thomas stuffed his riches back in his trouser pockets and said munificently, 'We can do anything you like!'

Lizzie was disappointed. 'I'd really like to go for a walk,' she said. This was the way she and Ace had planned it. There was a jeweller's shop on the way to the High Street, and it had a little gold chain with a gold Asterix pendant in the window. The pendant was just the same as Ivan

85

Prihoda's Asterix.

Falling in with Lizzie's wishes, Thomas Huber walked down the road with her. The wind was cold, a few drops of rain were falling, and there were several snowflakes among them. Lizzie was bare-headed. Thomas offered her his fur cap. Lizzie refused it. Just before they reached the jeweller's shop, Thomas wanted to cross the road, because there was a sports shop on the other side, and he was greatly interested in skis and ski boots.

'We can look at your skis on the way back,' said Lizzie, marching Thomas on up to the jeweller's window. 'Oh, look, isn't it lovely! I'd simply love one of those!' she cried, acting tremendously enthusiastic and pressing her nose to the plate glass window as she pointed to the golden Asterix on display. 'I've been wanting one for ages, but my mum won't buy me one!' she added. 'I'd give just *anything* for one of those pendants!'

'I say,' said Thomas, rather hesitantly, 'if you want one all that badly I can give you one. But you mustn't tell anyone, okay? It's got to be a secret?'

'Is it really just like that one? Gold, with enamel on the front of it?' Thomas nodded, and Lizzie felt like a hound just catching up with the fox.

'Had it ever since I was born,' said Thomas, 'but I don't like it all that much.'

Oh yes, thought Lizzie, ever since he was born? I've got him now! Asterix hasn't been going that long, has he? And it has to be a secret! Well, of course it does! If you're giving away stolen goods you don't want to broadcast the fact!

'I'll bring it to school tomorrow,' said Thomas Huber, and Lizzie felt very excited indeed. The case would be solved tomorrow! Thomas would hand over the Asterix pendant on the sly, she'd show it to Ivan, he'd swear it was his, and Thomas Huber would go white in the face and tell all. And on Monday His Nibs could come back to school again, head held high, cleared of all suspicion!

Just as Lizzie's visions of the future had reached this point, Thomas Huber added a little uncertainly, 'Only mine hasn't got that sky-blue cloud behind it. You don't mind about that, do you?'

Cloud? What cloud? Lizzie stared at the window. Why is he going on about a sky-blue cloud, Lizzie wondered, and then she noticed a pendant of a guardian angel lying right beside the Asterix pendant. The angel pendant showed the head of a cherub with little pink wings hovering in a sky-blue cloud.

Lizzie was so disappointed she could have wept. She choked back her tears, and said, 'No, Thomas, you can't give me your angel. I'm sure golden guardian angels are awfully expensive, and my mother doesn't like me to accept expensive presents.'

'That's why I thought we ought to keep it secret,' agreed Thomas. 'My mother would be pretty cross if she knew I'd given it away, too.'

'Well, if it's got to be a secret I can't wear the pendant, so there's no point in it.'

Thomas could see that. Indeed, he looked a little relieved. 'Shall we go on?' he asked.

Lizzie nodded glumly. They walked slowly down the street and turned into the road where Susi Kratochwil lived. As they passed the house, Lizzie asked casually, 'Did you enjoy Susi's party?'

'Yes, it was great!' said Thomas. 'Except you wouldn't take much notice of me! And it was a shame about the savings book, of course!'

'Well, why did she leave the savings books lying about, silly thing?' said Lizzie. 'Brainbox agrees with me—he says it's at least half her own fault. You ought to lock valuable things up!'

'Well, she did,' said Thomas Huber. 'After she showed us the savings books she put them back in their cupboard and locked it, and then she put the key away in the bottom drawer of that big desk!'

Lizzie tried to look bored, and as if she weren't interested, but she was thinking: I've got him this time! Clear as anything! I've talked to everyone in the class about that stolen savings book, and I kept saying you shouldn't leave such valuable things lying about, and nobody's contradicted me! Because nobody knew Susi *did* lock them up again. Even Susi herself didn't remember. She thought she'd left the key in the keyhole too! But of course the thief knows what she did with it all right! It meant a lot, to him!

'Only I wouldn't have expected Nibs to be quite so silly,' Thomas went on. 'I mean, it's stupid to think you can just draw money out of a savings book with a codeword!'

'*You'd* have known, though, wouldn't you?' There was a nasty, spiteful note in Lizzie's voice, but Thomas didn't seem to notice.

'You bet!' he said. 'For one thing, any fool knows! For another, I'm more likely to know than most. My dad works in a savings bank, so I know all sorts of stuff about banking, not just dead easy things like that!'

Lizzie gave up! She'd had enough of this—it was pointless. No, a boy with a father who works in a bank would *not* be such a fool as to steal a savings book with a codeword! Of course he wouldn't! Ace might have thought of that one himself!

'Look, Thomas,' said Lizzie, 'I haven't got any time just now. I've got to go, I'm afraid. Sorry!'

'Let's go into the café and have an ice, at least,' begged Thomas Huber.

'I think I *have* got a cold after all,' said Lizzie. 'An ice

88

wouldn't do it any good.'

Thomas Huber looked disappointed. 'What about the cinema?'

Lizzie didn't want to go to the cinema either. Lizzie wanted to go and see Ace and tell him Operation Huber was a flop. Ace lived quite close to here, by the crossroads. 'I can't go to the cinema,' said Lizzie. 'I'd probably sneeze all the time and bother people, with my cold. And anyway I've just remembered I've got to go and see my grandmother. It's urgent. She's ill.' And Lizzie turned and made for the crossroads and the building where Ace lived.

She stopped when she reached its front door. 'See you, then,' she said, and waited for Thomas to walk off. Thomas Huber looked incredulous.

'Your *grandmother* lives in here?' he said. 'Hey, this is where silly Ass lives!'

'Well? Can't my grandmother live in the same apartment building as Ace?' Lizzie would have liked to march straight in without another word to Thomas, but unfortunately the front door of the building was locked. There were three doorbells in a little niche beside the loudspeaker of the intercom device, with names beside them. One said EL-TERLEIN, another said ALOIS STINGL—*massage,* and the third said HUMPELSTETTER. Thomas Huber looked at the names. Everyone in these parts knew that Humpelstetter was quite a famous artist. You sometimes read about him in the gossip columns of the papers, when he left one woman and started living with another, but Lizzie's grandmother was unlikely to be the artist Humpelstetter's new inamorata. Nor was she a masseur called Alois Stingl.

'You're making it up,' said Thomas Huber, sadly. 'You're just making it all up. Why did you say you'd go out with me at all if you don't like me?' And Thomas Huber pressed the bell labelled ELTERLEIN.

'Hullo, who is it?' asked Ace's voice, through the loud-speaker.

'Visitor for you, silly Ass!' said Thomas Huber, and then he marched off.

The front door of the building hummed and clicked, and Lizzie pushed it open and went in, feeling she had behaved rather shabbily.

Ace stuck obstinately to his guns. Lizzie spent over an hour explaining why it looked as if Thomas Huber couldn't be the thief after all and saying she'd swear he was innocent. But Ace simply shook his head and said, 'He did it all right! He's just pretending! I tell you, he did it—he's really cunning! But I'll outwit him yet, it'll all come out. He won't get around *me*!'

At this point Lizzie rang Brainbox, to ask for his aid and support. She knew he had more influence on Ace than she did. Ace almost never argued with Brainbox. However, Brainbox wasn't at home. His mother said he had gone to the zoo, with His Nibs and Nibs's mother. She also said she wasn't too happy about it, she didn't like her son going around with thieves, and then the air of the zoo buildings always smelt so bad in winter, too. Lizzie couldn't bear to listen to any more of this. She just said, 'I'm sorry I bothered you,' and hung up. Then she tried ringing His Nibs at *his* home. They might both be back from the zoo. But nobody answered the Tabors' phone.

Ace wanted to play snap or dominoes with Lizzie, or teach her how to play chess. But Lizzie didn't feel like any of these games. 'I'm going home,' she said.

'Okay,' said Ace. 'I'll stay here and think. I'll think of a way to prove Thomas Huber's guilty.' He grinned. 'You just wait—I *can* think, you know! Brainbox isn't the only one around here who's good at thinking. I can do it too if I like!'

'Best of luck,' said Lizzie, all but adding, 'you silly ass!' Then, crossly, she went home.

It was seven-thirty in the evening, and Lizzie's mother and father were sitting in the living room watching the news on television, when the doorbell rang. Lizzie, who was sitting in her room learning English vocabulary, went out into the hall. 'Look through the peephole first, Lizzie!' called her mother, from the living room.

Lizzie obediently looked through the peephole, and saw Brainbox and Ace standing outside the apartment door.

'Who is it?' called her father.

'Brainbox and Ace,' said Lizzie. She unhooked the safety chain on the door, turned the key in the top lock, turned the key in the bottom lock, and opened the door itself.

'Like getting into Fort Knox,' said Brainbox, coming in. Ace followed him, grinning.

'What's up?' asked Lizzie, softly. For obviously there was *something* up: something important. Brainbox and Ace wouldn't come round at this time of day without some special reason. Lizzie took them both into her room, and her mother, who was terribly inquisitive besides being a terrible worrier, came out into the hall to polish up the big mirror on the wall near the door of Lizzie's room, However, her eavesdropping left her very little the wiser. She heard her daughter say, in surprise, 'What's that?' Then Ace said, proudly, 'The handkerchief!' Then Lizzie's voice, again: 'It's filthy!' To which Ace replied, 'That's because we used it to wipe the board.'

At this point Lizzie's mother went back into the living room, telling herself: well, I'm not going to shine up a mirror that's perfectly shiny already just to overhear a boring conversation about a dirty handkerchief!

Inside her room, Lizzie was sitting looking at the brown

91

and white check handkerchief that had been wrapped round Johanna Dohnal's watch. It was spread out on her desk, and she was staring at one corner of it. There was a monogram embroidered in the corner, consisting of the letters H and T.

'The moment you'd gone I realized the handkerchief could be important,' Ace told her. 'It's our only piece of evidence, right? So I wanted to put it somewhere safe. I couldn't remember where it actually was at first. In fact I thought someone might have thrown it away. Then I remembered Babsi Binder used it to wipe the board. So I went up to school and told the caretaker I needed the key to the classroom because I'd left my last packet of asthma tablets in my desk—'

'Asthma tablets? You mean you've got asthma?' Lizzie looked at Ace in alarm.

'He only said so to get into the classroom,' said Brainbox.

Ace nodded. 'And thank goodness it was still there! So now we've got our proof. T.H.—it proves Thomas Huber did it!'

Lizzie went on staring at the dirty handkerchief. It was a big one. The checks were rather washed out and the cotton was wearing thin. The letters of the monogram were embroidered in brown. They were rather squiggly, but they were definitely a T and an H. T as in Thomas and H as in Huber.

'Told you so all along!' Ace was jubilant. 'I can always rely on my feelings! Clear as crystal, right?'

Lizzie looked at Brainbox. He shrugged his shoulders. 'It *looks* like pretty clear proof,' he said. 'I did have a different theory, but that monogram's scuppered it.'

'What was your theory?' asked Lizzie.

'Never mind his theory,' said Ace, before Brainbox could answer her. 'His theory can go take a running jump! Proof, that's what counts!' Ace picked up the handkerchief, shook the chalk dust out of it, and spread it out on the desk again. 'I'm going to go and see the Head tomorrow morning and show him the monogram!'

Lizzie was surprised to find herself feeling sorry for Thomas Huber. She felt her heart sink in sympathy when she thought of Thomas facing the Headmaster tomorrow. That same Thomas who had been prepared to give her his guardian angel.

'Sorry for him, are you?' said Ace. Evidently he could read Lizzie's thoughts like a book. She was just about to say there was nothing actually wrong with feeling sorry for Thomas when the door opened, and her mother came in. She came in out of sheer curiosity, though she was not going to admit to it, so she asked if anyone wanted a coke. All three children said no. They did not feel like coke just at present. However, there was no holding Lizzie's mother now. If the boys had really come about a dirty handkerchief, she said to herself, it must be a very special handkerchief. Then she saw it, lying on Lizzie's desk. She went over to the desk, smiling. 'Goodness, whose old grandpa's hanky is that?'

As nobody answered her, Lizzie's mother left the room again, but Brainbox, watching her go, put his thumb in his mouth and murmured, 'A highly intelligent woman!'

Lizzie thought Brainbox was laughing at her mother. 'Well, yours won't be winning any Nobel prizes either!' she snapped. Brainbox picked up the handkerchief, folded it, and put it in his trouser pocket.

'Hey, you leave that alone!' said Ace. 'I found it! I'm taking it to the Head!' He looked as outraged as if someone were trying to cheat him out of a winning lottery ticket. 'Give me my evidence back at once!'

This, however, Brainbox refused to do. He said Lizzie's

mother had pointed him in the right direction, and he wanted the coming weekend to do some detective work.

'If I haven't found the thief by Monday,' he told Ace, 'you can have the handkerchief back then and take it to the Head.'

Ace was furious. He said Brainbox was totally pigheaded, and thick as two short planks, and the case was perfectly clear, only a raving lunatic could have any doubts about it now.

Brainbox persisted in his pigheadedness. He said he had better things to do than sit around here quarrelling, and he had a right, on the grounds of their ancient and long-standing friendship, to ask Ace to respect his wishes and put off going to the Head for a couple of days.

'And what about poor Nibs?' shouted Ace. 'I suppose you don't care about *him*! Just think how glad *he'd* be to be cleared tomorrow! Why should poor Nibs have to look like a thief all weekend?'

'Listen,' said Brainbox, with what, for him, was unusual forcefulness, 'Nibs will go along with anything I say!' And he placed considerable emphasis on the word 'I'. 'If you don't believe me, Ace, ring him up.'

'Okay, okay,' muttered Ace, who knew Brainbox was only telling the truth. 'All right, I'll wait till Monday. But not a moment longer!'

'You can do what you like on Monday, Ace,' said Brainbox, poking Ace in the chest with his forefinger. 'By Monday you'll be thanking me you didn't make a fool of yourself, going to the Head!' And he told Lizzie, 'Give your mum my love! I might have given up but for her, bless her heart!' Then he said goodbye and went home.

Ace and Lizzie stared at the door for quite a while after it had closed behind him.

'What exactly did your mum say, then?' asked Ace. 'Was

there anything special about it?'

'Nothing whatsoever!' said Lizzie, and added, after a moment, 'But I suppose Brainbox knows what he's doing. I mean, he always *does* know. *I* trust him, anyway!'

Ace didn't want to hang around Lizzie's place any longer. He said goodbye, rather coolly. And when he was outside the apartment, and Lizzie had turned the key in the door twice after him and hooked the chain across it, he murmured to himself, 'I ask you! He's got the entire lot of them right under his thumb!'

Chapter 11

in which we start with further extracts from Brainbox's diary, and then the story takes a turn calling for muscular as well as mental exertion on Brainbox's part.

Friday, December 3rd, 10.10 p.m.
I've washed the handkerchief, dried it on the radiator, ironed it and folded it neatly. Now it's sitting in front of me, monogram upwards. I've also decided not to be angry with anyone in 3D for suspecting His Nibs any more. Or in all fairness I'd have to be angry with Ace for suspecting Thomas Huber too. Says he can rely on his feelings. Feelings! Idiot! Let him rely on his feelings when it comes to whether or not he's got room for another of the great thick sandwiches he brings to school for break, fine, but he ought to leave his feelings out of it when other people are concerned. If FEELINGS are going to land other people in the soup I'd rather not have any! I mean, it's crazy! Just try tracing it all back . . . .

Thomas Huber gets a FEELING. It's a feeling of love for Lizzie. But Lizzie doesn't get the same sort of feeling. She has a FEELING of friendship for Ace. That upsets Thomas. He gets a FEELING of anger with Ace and so he keeps calling him Ass. This gives Ace a FEELING of hatred for Thomas, plus a FEELING that he's a thief, the first moment he gets any excuse. And instead of using his brain to try and work out what his FEELINGS are up to, he just uses it to think things that say his FEELINGS are quite right. And the idiot says he wants to study law some day! Let's just hope he gets to be a solicitor or something and not a judge, or he'll be laying down the law according to his silly FEELINGS!

But I'm more bothered about Nibs than Ace just now, and Nibs is in a pretty bad way. At the zoo today, he told me he didn't think he'd ever really be all right again, not the way he was before. Even when I find the real thief. He said, 'It won't change the way they all thought I was a thief and stopped being friends with me.' He's right, too.

And now I've got to make sure Ace keeps his silly mouth shut at school tomorrow, and doesn't go spreading his daft theory, or Thomas Huber will be in a bad way too, just like His Nibs.

Actually I don't think that will be difficult, because nobody else is talking to us much anyway. And we'll only have two lessons instead of four, because the art teacher's away sick, so there's no double art period, and that means only one break. And I'll use break to tell Lizzie and Ace my plan. School will be over at ten, because of no art, and then I've got the rest of the weekend. I'll start detecting directly, and I'll take Lizzie with me. It'll be easier with two of us.

And when all this is over I'll buy Lizzie's mum three red roses. If she hadn't said that, about an old grandpa's hanky, it might have been ages before it struck me that it's a very old handkerchief, and children don't often have huge check hankies with squiggly monograms embroidered in the corners. And in most families you just grab the first handkerchief that comes to hand. I've usually got one in my pocket with AA embroidered on it, because my mother's name is Annaliese Ammerling.

I'm worn out. I'm going to sleep now. I'll need good strong nerves tomorrow.

P.S. I just thought I ought really to take Ace with me, as well as Lizzie. I may be feeling a bit annoyed with him at the moment, but we're still friends. If I don't take him along, he'll feel left out. It'd be like saying yah boo, you made a mistake, you picked the wrong person as the thief so we don't want you any more!

School began at eight o'clock on Saturday, as usual, but it was over just before ten because of the absent art teacher. Brainbox, Ace and Lizzie dashed out of the building at five to ten. They were still wearing the old plimsolls which were their school indoor shoes, they had not buttoned up their jackets, their caps were in their jacket pockets, and they had left their satchels down in the cloakroom, much to the surprise of the rest of 3D, who were getting changed in the monkey cage at their leisure.

'Every moment counts!' Brainbox had told Lizzie and Ace. 'We've got to get there before him!'

'He walks home,' said Lizzie. 'If we take the tram we'll have a really good start!'

All Ace had said, under his breath, was, 'I don't believe it. I just do not believe it.' All the same, he led their dash to the tram stop, waving frantically at the driver of the tram that was just drawing up. The driver was a kind man. He waited for Ace to get there, he waited for Lizzie to clamber up on the step, he even asked, 'How about your fat friend? Coming too, is he?'

The kind driver did not start off again until Brainbox, puffing and panting, had hauled himself up into the tram with his last ounce of strength. 'Oh, my dear sweet heavens!' groaned Brainbox, collapsing on an empty seat and breathing stertorously. He was unable to do anything but wheeze and gasp and rattle until they got out two stops farther on.

There was a large supermarket with a small park beside it at the stop where the three of them got off. Beyond the park stood some new tower blocks, with balconies in front of the apartments, and several rows of older houses with tiny gardens. There was a very strong wind. The little birch trees in the park were shivering even more than Lizzie, whose teeth were chattering. 'So where's it supposed to be?' she asked.

Ace did up the zip of his anorak, put his woolly hat on, and muttered, 'Lives at the back of beyond, doesn't he?'

Brainbox took a piece of paper out of his pocket. 'Number 13, 26 Alois Rapottensteiner Way,' he read out loud. There was a sketch map on the piece of paper too, showing the supermarket, the tower blocks and the rows of houses. There was a little cross behind the farthest tower block. Lizzie looked at the piece of paper. 'Where'd you get it?'

'Got the address out of the telephone book,' said Brainbox. 'I spent ages on the phone yesterday, but nobody in 3D knew his address. And I copied the map off the big city map of Vienna.'

Brainbox, Lizzie and Ace made for the farthest tower block. 'Suppose his mother's not at home?' asked Lizzie.

'That's our bad luck,' said Ace.

'Who's going to ring the bell?' asked Lizzie.

'Ace,' said Brainbox. 'He's the best at putting on an act.'

They marched on in silence until they reached the entrance of the tower block. They went inside and found the lift. Lizzie pressed the red button. They waited for the lift to come down to the ground floor, Brainbox opened the door and Lizzie got in. Ace, however, hesitated. 'She'll just chuck me out,' he said. 'I tell you, this whole thing is silly!'

Brainbox gave Ace a push, and Ace, who had not been expecting it, lost his balance and stumbled into the lift. 'Hey, Brainbox!' said Ace, astonished. 'Since when did *you* take to pushing people around?'

'Since I stopped being my usual self at all,' muttered Brainbox, stepping into the lift himself. He let the door close and pressed the top button, beside the number 13.

As the lift went up, he handed Ace the handkerchief. 'Got it all straight?' he asked. Ace nodded. When they stopped at the thirteenth floor, he said, 'I'm only doing it out of friendship, mind. So you'll see how wide of the mark you are. Get it?'

'You can tell me all about your motives later,' whispered Brainbox, opening the door of the lift. Ace reluctantly stepped out into the corridor. There were three white doors,

99

with glass peepholes and nameplates behind them. The nameplate on the door opposite the lift said HAHN.

Ace and Lizzie went down the stairs built around the lift to the mezzanine floor just below. They sat on the bottom step of the flight and waited. They could hear Ace ringing the Hahns' bell on the floor above. Lizzie was so excited that she put two fingers in her mouth and bit their nails, a bad habit she had given up ages ago. 'There's nobody in,' she whispered.

'Wait a minute,' Brainbox whispered back. 'It may be a big apartment, or his mother's in the lavatory or something!'

The lift was going down again. Ace came to the top of the flight of stairs. 'Shall I ring again?' he asked.

'No, don't bother,' said Brainbox, standing up. 'Just our luck.' He knocked the dust of the staircase off the seat of his trousers.

'She could be in the supermarket,' said Lizzie. 'Most people's mums go to the supermarket on Saturday.'

'Women can spend hours in the supermarket,' said Ace. 'Wolfgang will get home long before her!'

Down below, they heard the lift door close, and then the creaking, buzzing sound of the lift cage making its way up again. Brainbox put a finger to his lips. When he realized it was coming up and up, not stopping at the eleventh floor, not stopping at the twelfth floor either, he waved frantically at Ace, and Ace went back to the door of the Hahns' apartment and rang the bell again.

'Hullo, did you want someone here?' The woman who had got out of the lift put two shopping bags down on the floor and got a key-ring out of one of them.

'Yes, please,' said Ace. 'Can I see Wolfgang?'

'Why, he's at school! School isn't over till twelve,' said the woman. She sounded surprised.

'Oh, I quite forgot,' said Ace. 'I go to a boarding school, you see and we get all Saturday off. I'm a friend of Wolfi's. We were in the same class last year. Before I went to the boarding school, I mean.'

The woman unlocked the door of the apartment. She seemed to be wondering whether to stay out in the corridor with her visitor or ask him in.

'I really only came because I've still got one of his handkerchiefs,' said Ace. 'He lent it to me when I had a cold, and I wanted to bring it back.'

'A handkerchief? You came just to return a handkerchief?'

Ace made one of his silliest faces. 'My mother says you have to be scrupulously honest with other people's property.'

'Yes, well, I see,' said the woman. She picked up her shopping bags again and nudged the door open with her foot.

'Only the thing is,' said Ace, squinting slightly by now, too, 'the thing is, I'm not quite sure the handkerchief really *is* Wolfi's.' And he showed her the brown and white check handkerchief with the monogram. She looked at it. 'Oh yes,' she said, smiling, 'that's one of ours. T.H. for Tassilo Hahn—that was my late father-in-law. He always used huge check handkerchiefs like that. Thank you so much!' The woman took the handkerchief, and as Ace was still standing there squinting and making his silly face, she asked, 'Would you like to come in?'

'Yes, please,' said Ace, and the door closed behind him.

Lizzie took her fingers out of her mouth. 'Well *done*, Brainbox!' she said. 'Come on, though, we'd better get out of here. Wolfgang will be back any minute!'

Brainbox nodded. They both ran downstairs to the main entrance of the building, where they took up their positions,

Brainbox on one side of it and Lizzie on the other. Brainbox had insisted that the first thing they must do was ask Wolfgang Hahn *why* he stole things. And whatever they did, they mustn't ask him in front of his mother.

Lizzie and Brainbox had not been standing outside the door of the building very long before Lizzie said, 'There he is! I recognize his pea-green anorak!'

'I'm a bit scared,' said Brainbox.

'Scared of Wolfgang Hahn?' Lizzie laughed. 'Oh, come on! He's wet and *feeble*!'

Brainbox put his thumb in his mouth and sucked it like the stem of a pipe. 'Not that sort of scared,' he said. 'I'm scared of what'll happen when the others shove their oar in.'

But Lizzie was not listening. She had been watching the pea-green dot attentively as it passed the supermarket, came closer, and turned recognizably into Wolfgang Hahn. 'Look!' she said excitedly. 'What's he doing? Where's he going now?'

For Wolfgang Hahn was not continuing on his way towards the tower blocks. Wolfgang Hahn was crossing the street and making for the rows of older houses. He turned off down the alleyway between the second and third rows, and Brainbox and Lizzie lost sight of him.

'Oh, *bother*,' said Lizzie. 'Do you think he saw us?'

'No, I don't,' said Brainbox. 'He's just taking time off. Because school was over two hours early.'

'But we can't wait here till twelve!' Lizzie looked at her battered plimsolls. 'My toes are frozen. I can't even feel them any more!'

At this moment Ace came out of the door of the building, looking crestfallen. 'Okay, you win, Brainbox,' he said. 'I'd never have thought it. I swear, I'd never have thought it.' And he told the other two that Wolfgang's mother had not only given him a Coke, she had shown him a whole pile of check handkerchiefs that had belonged to her father-in-law. 'Proof positive Wolfi did it,' said Ace. 'Proof absolutely positive!'

'And now he's gone and given us the slip,' said Lizzie, pointing to the old houses. 'He went off there somewhere. In between the second and third rows.'

'He's got a friend there,' said Ace. 'His mother told me. She's nice. She told me how he found a friend at last. He used to be very sad, she said, because he didn't make friends at school, and supposedly nobody at school would talk to him—'

'What do you mean, supposedly?' asked Brainbox, interrupting. 'It's perfectly true. Nobody likes him much.'

'Well, anyway, he made friends with somebody a couple of weeks ago,' Ace went on, 'and now apparently he's happy. So his mother's happy too.'

'Somebody in our class, you mean?' asked Lizzie.

'No, this friend is two years older than Wolfi, or so Wolfi told his mother, and he lives in one of those old houses. She doesn't know too much about it herself. This friend only moved in a few weeks ago. Wolfi met him on the recreation ground, and now they're inseparable.'

'How on earth did you get all this out of Wolfgang's mother?' asked Brainbox, surprised.

Ace smiled. 'I didn't have to *get* it out of her, she told me all about it of her own accord. I made out I was an old friend of his, you see, and so she said that just went to show poor Wolfi was only imagining things, and he did have friends, and people in the class liked him after all. And so on. And she asked me why I hadn't been to see him before, because Wolfi was always moping about at home on his own. So I said I'd like to come and see him another time, if that was how he felt, I said I'd be glad to—well, of course I didn't mean it—and *then* she said he had another friend too, and that was how it started.' Ace smiled. 'She'd have told me her whole life story if I hadn't got up to go!' He blew his nose. 'Well, come on, let's go and find the friend's house!' he said, stuffing his handkerchief back in his pocket, and he started off.

Brainbox went after him and grabbed his sleeve. 'Hang on!' he said. 'There must be a couple of hundred houses there. Are you planning to ring every single doorbell?'

'Why not?' said Ace, without stopping. 'I'll ring bells till I fetch the mice up out of the cellars if I have to!' And he went on walking very fast. Much faster than Brainbox could go. Brainbox dropped behind.

Lizzie could have kept up with Ace all right, but she decided to slow down to Brainbox's pace. 'Let him!' she said. 'He'll soon find out it's no good asking about someone if you don't know his name or what he looks like!'

Brainbox nodded, and walked on, panting.

When he and Lizzie turned into the alleyway between the second and third rows of houses, Ace was standing there talking to an old man. The old man was pointing down the road.

'Whether they have a lad or not, couldn't rightly say,' he was telling Ace. 'Somebody moved in there a few weeks back, though. I saw the furniture van.' The old man put two fingers to his mouth and whistled, and an extremely fat dog with crooked little legs and a great many bald patches on its coat came waddling up and sniffed at the legs of Ace's jeans. 'Plenty of furniture vans around, of course,' added the old man. 'Folk keep buying new furniture. But there was some old stuff too came out of the van down there.'

'On the right or the left of the street?' asked Ace.

'Down there on the right,' said the old man.

'What number, do you know?'

'Place where Frau Prowaznik used to live,' said the old

104

man. The fat dog had had enough of sniffing at Ace's jeans. It waddled over to a garden gate and barked.

'Why d'you want to know all this?' asked the old man.

'Oh, he's an old friend of mine,' said Ace, and could have bitten his tongue off next moment, for the old man shot him a suspicious glance.

'Old friend of yours, and you don't know his name?' he said. 'Nor what he looks like? Don't you try fooling me, my lad!' The old man turned and made for the garden gate where the fat dog was waiting. Ace started off after him, but the old man shouted, 'Get away, boy, or I'll set the dog on you!' And he disappeared into his house as fast as he could. The fat dog stayed in the garden, barking angrily.

Brainbox and Lizzie joined Ace. 'Well, at least we know to try the bottom right-hand half of the street,' said Brainbox.

'And just where do you suppose the bottom right-hand half begins?' said Lizzie, so cold by now that her teeth chattered when she spoke. Brainbox decided that when the old man said, 'Down there on the right,' he had meant somewhere past the big bottle bank standing by the roadside. And Ace decided there was no point the three of them going around together, like We Three Kings of Orient Are, asking after the whereabouts of a child. 'Let's split up and knock at different doors,' he suggested. 'I'll start with Number 24!'

'I'll try the house with the garden gnome,' said Lizzie, pointing to Number 30.

Ace fished in his pocket and produced a Red Cross lottery ticket. 'I'll ring the bell and offer them this ticket, and then I'll—well, I'll turn on the charm, and spy around a bit!'

'I think I'll just ask about Frau Prowaznik,' said Lizzie. 'After all, there's no reason I should know she doesn't live here any more!'

Brainbox pointed down the street. 'I'll go down there and look at the names on the garden gates,' he said.

Ace objected, saying Brainbox just wanted to get out of the hard work of ringing bells and asking questions. 'You daren't!' he said. 'Go on, admit it!'

'Bet you I find the house, all the same,' said Brainbox, smiling. Ace had already lost several similar bets with Brainbox, so he said no more, and marched down the garden path of Number 24. Lizzie went on down the road with Brainbox until she got to the garden gnome at Number 30. Then Brainbox went on by himself. He carefully inspected the names on the garden gates. Muller, Meier, Springer—but it wasn't the names that actually interested him. He was examining the condition of the nameplates, looking for a brand new one. Somebody who only moved in a couple of weeks ago won't have a grotty old nameplate with rusty screws in it, thought Brainbox. The lettering won't be the squiggly old-fashioned sort either, and the paint won't be wearing off the letters. And if the nameplate's made of enamel there won't be any cracks in it.

Brainbox found his brand new nameplate at Number 38. It said CONRAD WEITRA: ENGINEER, in nice new letters engraved on a small brass plate. Brainbox went on to the end of the row, just in case, right down to Number 50, but none of the other gates had a new nameplate on them. So he turned round and went back to the fence outside Number 38.

Lizzie was coming out of the garden with the gnome in it. She ran towards him. 'Frau Prowaznik lived at Number 38!' she called. When she reached Brainbox, she realized he was standing outside that very house. She looked at him in awe and amazement, but she got no chance to express her awe and amazement in words, because Ace was just coming out of the garden of Number 24, running to join them. 'It's either thirty-six or thirty-eight!' he called. He had something long wrapped in white paper under his arm.

'Here I am, as the tortoise told the hare,' said Brainbox, grinning.

'What on earth's that?' asked Lizzie, pointing to the object under Ace's arm.

'A Christmas yeast cake,' said Ace. 'The old woman in there has a whole cupboard full of them, and she's starting another batch of dough right now, and she's got nobody to give them to, she said. Crazy! I almost got landed with another one!'

'Phew—I hope I don't live to be really old,' said Brainbox, and then he sighed, and made for the garden gate.

'Are you just going to walk in?' asked Lizzie. Brainbox nodded.

The garden gate was not locked. The three of them walked down a narrow concrete path towards the house, in single file: Brainbox first, then Lizzie, and Ace bringing up the rear. The door of the house was painted green. They could hear music coming out of the house, and it was very loud by the time they reached the door.

'The old lady with the yeast cakes said the boy who moved in here is very tall and fat,' said Ace, 'and he's often at home in the mornings. She once asked him if he didn't have to go to school, and he put his tongue out at her!'

'The woman *I* saw said I wouldn't have any luck asking for Frau Prowaznik around here,' said Lizzie, 'because she'd moved away and there was never anyone in this house except that stupid boy. She said his father's working abroad somewhere, and his mother runs a coffee bar, so she's almost never there. She doesn't come home till midnight or later.'

Brainbox tried the handle of the green door. He was not really expecting it to open, but it did. The door was not locked.

107

There was a hall on the other side of it, and Wolfgang's pea-green jacket was hanging on a hook in the hall. A wooden spiral staircase led to the first floor, and there were four more doors in the hall as well as the front door. The doors were newly painted. One of them had a little plate on it with a picture of a baby: a boy baby spending a penny. There was another little plate on the door next to it, except that this one had a picture of a saucepan and two wooden spoons instead.

'So they don't get the kitchen and the lavatory mixed up,' said Ace, grinning.

The music they had heard while they were still outside the house was very loud now. It was coming from a door beside the wooden staircase, a door without any little doorplate on it.

Ace opened this door and saw a flight of steps leading down to the basement. Cautiously and quietly, the other two followed him down. They found themselves in a white-washed room lit by a naked light bulb. There was a red boiler here, and an oil tank in one corner. The place smelt of oil too. And there was another door: a grey metal door, with the words CONRAD WEITRA JUNIOR written on it in huge letters with thick red felt pen. A notice saying NO ENTRY was glued underneath, and there were several rows of pink stickers with black skulls and crossbones, the sort chemist's shops put on bottles with poisonous contents. By now the music was so loud it hurt Brainbox's ears, and Lizzie couldn't make out a word when he told her so.

There was neither handle nor lock on the metal door, only a bolt on the outside. It was standing ajar. Brainbox opened it, and saw a candle-lit basement room with a camp bed in it. A tall, fat boy was lying on this camp bed, and Wolfgang Hahn was sitting on an orange box beside it. He had a sheepskin jacket round his shoulders. Both he and the fat boy were smoking. There were posters of motorbikes and cowboys and naked girls round the walls of the room. The deafening music came from a record player, and there were four loudspeakers in the room.

Wolfgang Hahn was staring at the doorway in horror. It was impossible to say whether the fat boy was looking horrified too. Very fat faces are unable to express much.

Brainbox, Lizzie and Ace went into the basement room. There was a light switch on the wall beside the door. Brainbox flicked it on, and a powerful light bulb on the ceiling lit up. Ace went over to the record player and lifted the cartridge arm. Suddenly everything was perfectly quiet. Lizzie tugged at Brainbox's sleeve, indicating a huge poster of a fierce-looking cowboy, life-size, with a Colt in either hand, and a chain around his neck. A real chain. A gold chain with a gold Asterix pendant. Someone had made holes in the poster on both sides of the cowboy's neck and threaded the chain through the holes. And the cowboy had a pigskin purse stuck to his chest, apparently with all-purpose glue. Lizzie's purse. But the really crazy thing about the cowboy was his ammunition belt. It had fountain pens, ballpoint pens and several pairs of compasses dangling from it, crowded close together. Two of the ballpoints looked just like pens Ace had recently 'lost'. And there were large cardboard cartons up against the wall by the door, full of the most extraordinary collection of things: chocolate, chewing gum, electric batteries, gents' socks, erasers, packets of tights, cards of elastic, rolls of film, cakes of soap, packets of needles, combs and packets of biscuits. There were even little packets of herb seeds in those cardboard cartons.

The fat boy sat up on the camp bed. 'Hey, what are you lot doing? Get out!' He was balancing an ash tray on his stomach, and now he stubbed his cigarette out in it. Then he turned to Wolfi Hahn. 'Kid, show our visitors out!' he said, making what he meant to be a grand gesture in the direction of the door. 'They want to be on their way!' And he tried to assume an expression indicating that he was master of the situation, but failed. In so far as his fat face could show feelings, what it showed was fear. Nor did he quite manage to keep the alarm out of his voice when he went on, 'Go on, show them the door!'

Wolfi Hahn was very pale. His glasses had slipped down on his nose and the sheepskin had slipped off his shoulders. He had dropped his cigarette. He was wearing a home-made badge with a death's head on it and the number 2, pinned to the chest of his green sweater. In a shrill and birdlike voice, Wolfi Hahn squeaked, 'They're from my school!'

'You idiot!' The fat boy shot up. There was a badge on his own chest too, but it had the number 1 under the death's head. 'You stupid, cretinous halfwit!' he shouted. 'Why did you have to go and tell them about our HQ?'

Wolfi Hahn's lips were quivering and bloodless; they looked as pale as his face.

'Don't shout so, Fatty!' said Ace, picking up the end of the fat boy's camp bed and lifting it into the air. 'Keep quiet, will you, Podge?'

'I'll shout all I want! This is *my HQ—mine!* Get out, all of you!' roared the fat boy.

Ace raised the end of the camp bed a little higher and then jerked it upwards with all his might. The fat boy did a half somersault backwards off it, and lay there in a corner, holding his head and groaning.

'Did the two of you steal all those things?' Lizzie asked Wolfi Hahn.

'It wasn't stealing!' sobbed Wolfi. 'It was just tests—tests of courage.'

'And that walking tub of lard,' said Brainbox, pointing to

the fat boy, who was slowly sitting up, 'that great fat jug-eared balloon made you take these tests?'

'Everybody who wants to be in the gang's got to,' sobbed Wolfi.

'Everybody?' asked Brainbox, frowning. 'How many of you are there, then?'

'Only us two so far, but—'

The fat boy interrupted Wolfi. 'Shut up, you fool! It's none of their business!'

Ace went right up close to the fat boy and asked him whether he fancied turning another somersault, a forward one this time, and fetching up in a different corner of the basement. The fat boy looked furious. Just for a moment he seemed to be about to tackle Ace head on, but then he grinned. 'Okay! Want to come into the business, pardners?' And he grinned again, this time at Ace in particular. 'You can be my Number Two!'

Ace was speechless with surprise and fury. The fat boy misunderstood. 'Hand that badge over,' he told Wolfi Hahn. Wolfi clutched his death's head badge with both hands. 'I'm your Number Two, Conrad!' he wailed. 'I started the whole thing up with you!'

'You're a fool,' the fat boy told Wolfi, and then he turned back to Ace and said, in confidential tones, 'He's a right idiot! Can't do a thing right! Goes pinching the sort of savings book that needs you to know the codeword to get money out, the stupid fool!'

Ace slapped the fat boy's face so hard that his fingers left four red marks across his cheek. The fat boy overbalanced, and sat down in one of the big cartons, right in the middle of the mixed bag of goods it contained. He was stuck there in among the rolls of film and chocolate bars and biscuits, and couldn't get out. Wolfi came over to help him, but as soon as he got close enough the fat boy kicked out furiously with

III

both feet.

Lizzie had torn the chain with the Asterix pendant and her pigskin purse off the cowboy poster. 'What else have you got here from our class?' she asked. Hesitantly, Wolfi removed several ballpoint pens and fountain pens and a pair of compasses from the ammunition belt. 'The rest of them came from the supermarket,' he said in an undertone. The fat boy was still in the carton, making no attempt to get out of it. Wolfi Hahn took two scarves, a pocket diary and a pair of nail scissors out of a box. 'That's all, honest,' he said. 'The money's gone now.'

Lizzie laid these items on one of the scarves and bundled them up in it. 'Right,' she said. 'I suggest we get out of here and take Wolfi with us.'

'You're not going to let that stuck-up oaf there go, are you?' said Ace indignantly.

'He isn't actually *going* anywhere,' Lizzie pointed out. She indicated the tiny window right up near the ceiling. 'He can't get out of that—it's too small, and too high up, and it's got bars over it too. And there's a bolt on the outside of the door!'

At this point the fat boy began to struggle, flailing his arms and legs around and shouting, 'Wolfi, help me out of here!'

Wolfi Hahn was actually on his way to help him out of the carton, but Brainbox shoved him out of the door.

'Bye-bye, big boss!' said Ace, waving to the fat boy as he marched off.

'You've got enough to eat, anyway!' remarked Lizzie, before she left the basement herself. Then she slammed the door and shot the bolt.

'But he'll die of hunger and thirst in there!' sobbed Wolfi Hahn, as Brainbox hauled him up the steps. Tears were rolling down his cheeks. 'His mother sometimes doesn't come home till the small hours—and then she takes sleeping tablets and she doesn't hear a thing. Honest!'

'She'll notice he's missing some time!' said Ace.

They reached the hall. There was a small telephone table in between the door with the baby on it and the door with the saucepan on it, and a list of phone numbers hung on the wall behind the telephone. Someone had written a number at the bottom of the list, in a childish hand, with the words MUM: COFFEE BAR beside it.

'Wolfi's right,' said Brainbox. 'We can't just leave him down there!' And he picked up the receiver of the telephone and dialled the number beside MUM: COFFEE BAR. 'Please can I speak to Frau Weitra?' he asked, and a moment later he went on, 'Hullo, Frau Weitra. I'm here in your house. You don't actually know me, but I'm here with two of my friends, and I wanted to tell you we've shut your son in the basement. In the room with the metal door. You'll see why if you have a look around in there. I only wanted to say we're going now, and maybe you ought to come and see to your son, and we've got to leave the front door unlocked because there isn't any key!' And Brainbox put the receiver down. 'Well, she was staggered!' he told the others. 'It took her breath away—I could *hear* it being taken away, down the phone!' And he suddenly called out, 'Hey, you stay here!' and grabbed Wolfi Hahn's arm. Wolfi had been making for the door. He struggled, and kicked and bit and shouted and sobbed.

'Look, we only want to take you home to your mother and have a word with her,' said Brainbox. 'Don't make such a fuss!'

But at this Wolfi kicked and bit and shouted even harder. It was hard to make out exactly what he was shouting, except for the words, 'I'm not going home! Please don't tell my mum!' which were clearly audible.

Brainbox couldn't keep his grip on Wolfi Hahn. Wolfi tore himself free, even though he was so small and feeble. He almost managed to get out of the door, and he was already turning the handle when Ace grabbed him round the middle from behind. Wolfi kicked again, and tried to bite Ace, but his strength was almost gone.

'Don't be so silly!' Brainbox told him. 'Where else will you go if you don't go home? Do try to think straight!'

Lizzie took the pea-green jacket off its peg and offered it to Wolfi. 'We'll make it all right with your mother,' she said. 'Honestly. And we'll give the rest of the things back to the others. And I don't need my money back.'

Wolfi Hahn calmed down and stopped kicking. He stopped trying to bite, too, and Ace let go of him. He just stood there, sobbing quietly, and let Lizzie help him into the pea-green jacket. She found his glasses, which he had lost while kicking and biting, and put them on his nose. Brainbox took him by one arm and Ace took him by the other. 'We mustn't let him get away,' Brainbox whispered to Ace. 'He's quite capable of running off and doing himself an injury.' And Ace nodded.

Lizzie opened the front door of the house. Two policemen were coming up the narrow concrete path. There was a police car parked in the street outside the garden gate. And three women stood by the fence, staring curiously.

Chapter 12

in which there isn't any happy ending, because this sort of story can't have a happy ending unless its readers are so hard-hearted they aren't interested in anything except who dunnit. In which case they might as well take the arrival of the two policemen as the happy ending and put the book down at this point. For the less hard-hearted reader, however, here is a final extract from Brainbox's diary.

Sunday, December 5th
I feel awful.

We didn't manage to settle everything as quietly as I'd hoped. I mean, it simply never occurred to me the fat boy's mother might call the police! I thought she'd come home herself. It's my fault. I didn't explain things to her properly over the phone. If I'd told her she'd find a whole hoard of things stolen from school and the supermarket in her basement, and her fat son thought he was boss of the Death's Head Gang, I'm sure she wouldn't have called the police. But when the police turned up there was nothing for it: we had to tell them the whole story. They thought we were thieves and goodness knows what else at first—Lizzie and Ace and me, I mean.

That fat boy is pretty nearly the end, but his mother really is the end! She's ghastly. I never knew a mother could be that bad before. When she got to the police station she had to be forcibly restrained from beating fat Conrad up. And she acted as if she were the chief sufferer in the whole business. And she kept saying, 'Just wait till my husband hears about this!' and, 'I'll put him in a Home!' And she told the policemen and the social worker who was there all the things she'd bought her fat boy recently. 'He doesn't lack for anything! He gets everything he wants!' she kept shouting.

Wolfi Hahn's mother came to the police station too. She was quite different. She hardly said a thing. I think it took her a terribly long time to understand just what had happened. And it is *hard to understand*. I mean, I can just about make out why Wolfi Hahn did all the things he did. But how do you get to be a *person like fat Conrad?* I should think you'd have to live in a sort of way I can't quite imagine.

We're going to meet at His Nibs's place in half an hour's time, and we'll have to go over it all again for his benefit. We only phoned him yesterday, because we spent ages at the police station, and then we had to calm our mothers down. They thought something dreadful had happened to us, because we'd never come home from school. They all telephoned each other, and apparently my mother was even more upset than Lizzie's mother, which I can hardly imagine! And Ace's father swore he'd never be angry with his son again, if only he got him home safe and sound. Ace can't imagine that, either.

I expect His Nibs is quite glad things turned out the way they did. With the police, and everything all cleared up. But it wasn't meant to end that way. That's what we agreed—me and Nibs, I mean.

When I first suspected Wolfi Hahn must be the thief, I told Nibs. And I told him I didn't think Wolfi was stealing things just out of greed, I thought there was something much more complicated behind it. And it would probably turn out to be a rather sad story. So then Nibs came to a very noble decision. He said if I was right, we wouldn't go and tell everyone. We wouldn't tell the rest of the class. His Nibs said now he knew what they're like when they think someone's a thief, he wouldn't wish it on Wolfi Hahn. And it wouldn't make anything any better for the whole of 3D to be enjoying themselves saying how horrible Wolfi was. And anyway, said Nibs, he had to live with the sad feeling that nobody in the class except the three of us had stood by him, and that wouldn't go away even if he was completely cleared. And he despised the others now, and he didn't care at all if people he despised despised him back! He only wanted Dr Hufnagel to know the truth. He wanted her to know he hadn't done it, because he doesn't despise her, he loves her.

I thought this was a great decision for Nibs to make, *really* marvellous, and I was thrilled. But now I think it all over more calmly I have to admit it probably wouldn't have worked. Would Dr Hufnagel really have kept quiet if we told her? And wouldn't Nibs's patience have given way some time, if somebody said something stupid to him, and then the truth would have slipped out? And Wolfi Hahn would have had to depend on our goodwill, and he'd have been terrified we might tell after all, the whole time.

'You must just show him you like him, too,' my mother said today when I told her why Wolfi was so keen to be friends with fat Conrad and he'd do anything he said.

But that's just the trouble. We didn't like him before, and we don't like him now. Since I found out about him, I've been sorry for him, but that's not the same as liking him. He's boring and wet and not very bright. He doesn't even smell very nice, somehow.

I wish you could learn to like people. I don't mean just liking a few people because they've got blue eyes with black speckles in them, or they smell nice, or they're funny or clever. You ought to be able to say: not many people like so-and-so, he could do with being liked a bit, I'll like him!

I wonder if you can teach yourself to like people? With a lot of practice, and a lot of patience?

I suppose I could always try. But I have a kind of feeling I won't keep it up very long. He really doesn't smell very nice. And he's boring and stupid too. Even the way he keeps pushing his glasses up his nose gives me the shivers!

P.S. I'm off to see His Nibs now. And when we're all at his place I'll mention that, about liking people, only sort of casually—so it doesn't sound so lofty and moral and all. Maybe one of my friends will think the same way. If we could share out liking horrible Wolfi Hahn between us a bit, the whole thing would be much, much easier.